Dead Bird Thro

"Mystery-solving twins, a bird hater out of Macbeth, and lots of giggly wordplay -- good fun!"

—Richard Scrimger

"A zany and zippy follow up to *Dead Frog on the Porch*. Snoopy twins Cyd and Jane are on the hunt for a bird killer, but they expose an eco-conspiracy instead. Their over-the-top antics will have young readers laughing and clamouring for more. This delightful novel places author Jan Markley in the catbird seat among funny mystery writers."

—Marty Chan

Dead Frog on the Porch

"Shady scientists, fraudulent frogs, and two terrific twins add up to a delightful mystery. Cynthia and Jane are fearless in their quest to end 'crimes against amphibians.' This story is full of outsized characters, outrageous creatures and a sweet goofy humor that propels each page. Tons of fun!"

—Teresa Toten
Governor General Awards nominee 2001
Governor General Awards finalist 2006

"Readers who enjoy a good laugh and a good mystery will devour this uproarious, fast-paced story in which the feisty twin sisters Cyd and Jane take a megabyte out of crime! It is Nancy Drew for the iPod generation! Markley's début novel, filled with suspense and zany humour and told with pizzazz, ushers in a new voice in the mystery genre. A sure winner!"

—Shenaaz Nanji
Governor General Award Finalist 2008.

Dead Bird Through the Cat Door

A Megabyte Mystery
by Jan Markley

gumboot books
www.gumbootbooks.com

ISBN 978-1-926691-15-2 (print)

ISBN 978-1-926691-17-6 (electronic book text)

Library and Archives Canada Cataloguing in Publication

Markley, Jan, 1961-

    Dead bird through the cat door / Jan Markley.

ISBN 978-1-926691-15-2

    I. Title.

PS8626.A7537D41 2010   jC813'.6   C2010-907079-8

Cover Illustration by Mike Linton

Book Design by Crystal Stranaghan

With special thanks to Jared Hunt and Melanie Jackson for all their editorial guidance and advice.

www.gumbootbooks.com

Printed and bound in Canada on acid-free paper that contains no material from old-growth forests, using ink that is safe for children.

To all my nieces and nephews for offering their youthful, yet wise, advice over the years. JM

Chapter One
The First Bird

In a flash of feathers and fur Yin bolted through the cat door with a dead baby robin in her jaws. I trailed her as she ran down the stairs to the basement where she stood proudly beside the bird. Her whiskers stretched into a cat smile. The same look she gives me when she throws up a hairball in my shoes.

I couldn't help petting Yin as she purred at her accomplishment. "You are a menace to the bird population," I joked, as I scratched behind her ears.

I thought the only way Yin would be able to catch a bird was if it fell out of its nest and into her mouth. The baby robin's feathers were black from Yin's saliva and my stomach turned – that hatchling hadn't stood a chance.

"Cyd, you down there? Let's go."

Oh, carp! Hide the evidence. It's Jane. Images of her crying over her dead frog last summer flashed through my cranium.

"Yup, gotta clean something up. Be right...." But Jane was right there; right over my shoulder peering down at the dead bird I'd ditched into the laundry room garbage pail.

"Don't look." Of course, when you say don't look the first thing a kid does is look.

"Oh, no, a baby bird." Jane's tear ducts sprang a leak. She crouched down.

Jane was unlucky with animals, and we had the backyard pet cemetery to prove it. It was mostly pets, but now she could include wild baby robins – soon to be an endangered species of our backyard if Yin had anything to do with it.

"Cyd, why'd you let Yin out? There's a robin's nest in the apple tree this year. You knew that," she accused me through her tears.

"Me? I didn't know the cat door was open." I flipped through the book of excuses I kept in my mind – I had a million of them. "Besides, she's a cat. That's what they do. It's a present for us ... a dead present, but still a present."

Jane glared at me as her tear ducts sprang a second leak. I put my excuses on hold. I'd gone too far. I knelt beside her.

Yin crawled on to her lap and rubbed her head against Jane's chin. "Yin, you killed a bird." They both stared at the spot on the carpet that was now vacant of a dead bird. Yin looked like we should be presenting her with the Most Awesome Cat of the Year Award. Jane … not so much.

The silence … and purring were deafening.

"I guess we can cancel her subscription to *Pampered Indoor Cats that Live in the Lap Of Luxury*," I said.

"That's not a real magazine title."

"No, but it would be funny if it was. Maybe Yin could live in the wild, fend for herself."

"What would Yin do in the wild?" Jane asked. She rolled her eyes; she wasn't buying the whole Yin versus nature thing.

I tied up the plastic bag.

"Where are you going with that bag?" Jane asked as she wiped her eyes with the back of her hand.

"Garbage – in the back alley behind the garage, and then bike ride?" Jane could always read my mind. "What's up?"

"Cyd." She shot me the woeful eye look. "You can't just leave it in there with the dryer lint and fabric soft-ener sheets."

"Come on Jane, we don't even know this bird. It's not like it's one of our pets or something."

Jane didn't speak. She gave me the silent you-know-what-we-have-to-do treatment.

"All right, a proper burial. In the animal graveyard we call a backyard." I put the garbage pail down and stomped upstairs to the utility drawer. I yanked out a pair of disposable rubber gloves, the kind Mom uses in the lab or here at home when she's slicing up hot chilies. Now they were transporting-a-dead-baby-robin-to-its-final-resting-place gloves. "Why do I always have to bury it?" I clomped back down the stairs.

"I'll dig the hole and Yin will tell us a story about the bird."

"We're not five and this is not a pet hamster." I don't know why I was so mad. It wasn't the bird's fault. Jane threw me a look that reminded me of all the dead pets she'd buried and I checked my attitude. "Proper burial, I get it. Come on Yin, you ferocious jungle cat."

With a garden spade, Jane bee-lined it to the woody part of our backyard. It was like a miniature forest. Sunk into the ground, it was filled with trees, bushes and flowers. This is where we would sometimes write our mystery novel plots.

Jane dug and I tried to keep Yin from tearing open the bird carcass. I held the songbird in my hand high, and out of Yin's reach. When the hole was ready I placed the bird in and Jane covered it with dirt. The hole was dangerously close to the burial plot of the late Frogzilla, who I accidentally killed. That led us to solve a crime against the frog kingdom. Even though Jane forgave me and has Frogzilla the Sequel, she'll never forget.

Yin didn't have much to say over the grave other than a few well-placed meows. She was already scouting out her next kill.

"How about a bike ride?" I asked. It would take Jane's mind off the dead bird. The sun stayed up well past supper, but we get late afternoon storms. We needed to hit the bike trails early. With Yin in the house and the cat door secured we hit the long and dusty – trail that is. Actually, it was a paved path with lots of signs about the helmet law and the dog by-law. Lots of laws.

"How about we ride the trail by the Wildwood Bird Sanctuary?" Jane asked. "It will be a tribute to Chirpy."

"Who? What? Don't tell me you named the bird we just buried?" I asked.

"Okay, I won't tell ya. Next stop, bird sanctuary."

With that she sped off. I thought I was supposed to be the sarcastic twin.

Chapter Two
The Second Bird

Blog post title: *Hot pink bike shorts are not good camouflage.*

I learned that the hard way. Especially when you've just stumbled upon a new mystery. It was a blue sky, slightly-too-hot kinda day for a ride on the bike path through the bird sanctuary. Jane had skidded to a halt in front of me. That's when we landed up to our bird beaks in intrigue.

"Look, a lynx," Jane declared.

There were wild animals down here, mostly coyotes, foxes, and beavers, but a lynx. Now that was curious.

I squeezed on the brakes and almost toppled over the handlebars. A cat with no tail sashayed across the trail.

"No, it's just a house cat. A large house cat that enjoys her dinner."

A man in a lab coat and kilt, who flourished a butterfly net like a weapon, chased after the cat. Jane and I looked at each other, then peered in the direction of the cat-chasing man. "Now that was just weird," we said.

"Weirdiously mysterious," I added.

You didn't have to tell us twice. The dog days of summer would bark on endlessly without a new mystery to write about ... or solve.

I dragged my bike off the trail and ditched it in the woods.

"Technically, you're not allowed to have your bike off the path," Jane pointed out.

"Technically, a crazy dude isn't supposed to be wearing a lab coat and running around with a butterfly net," I snapped back.

Jane rolled her bike to the nearest bike lock-up post and fiddled with her key and chain. I was halfway through the woods on the footpath when I realized she wasn't following me. I slowed down and peered through the brush at the man. He stopped up ahead and scooped something up in his butterfly net.

I became one with the tree I hid behind and motioned to my twin Jane to zip her lip as we spied on the man in a skirt. He swished the butterfly net back and forth like he was playing tennis.

The trees of the river valley surrounded us and covered up the skyline of the buildings downtown. A shaft of light broke through the foliage and my hot pink bike shorts glowed. The neon lime green pair I had at home probably wouldn't be any better for undercover work. I bet Nancy Drew never had this problem. She always wore skirts and they were never hot pink or neon green. But we were modern girl detectives and writers.

I felt Jane behind me.

"What's happening?"

"Crazy dude who should be in a straitjacket, and not a lab coat, scooped up something in the net." Okay, Jane was up to speed. "Let's creep up," I whispered. We inched forward, and branches crunched underfoot. We were making too much noise but I scouted out a good spying spot behind a tree. Jane trailed close behind me.

He reached down with one arm and used it like a forklift to scoop up the large tailless cat. I saw him shift his weight. He groaned under the burden of fat and fur.

"Aye, my sweet, more black pudding for you. You caught a fat one here. One down, three thousand more to go," he chortled. The sound bounced off the trees and shattered the silence of the woods. He stroked the cat along her back, extending his arm to where the tail would be. Jane and I raised an eyebrow at each other.

"We must get back to Souris." He had some kind of an accent, Scottish, I think.

"Who is he talking about?" asked Jane.

"Crazy Scottish moustache guy talking to his cat about a mouse. I don't know. Shh, he's turning around."

"Soon I will only hear cranes."

Jane and I exchanged a *say what?* glance.

He walked toward us. His chest puffed up with his victory. I noticed, as the pleats of his kilt swayed back and forth as he lumbered, that his skinny, sunburned-birdlike legs were in contrast to his puffed up chest.

He was in a world of his own. The cat hitched up under one armpit and the butterfly net he held in the other hand hung over his shoulder. He sauntered by, crushing twigs and branches under his feet, and I caught a glimpse of what was in his net. I tensed up, and Jane's bony fingers dug into my shoulder. Those bony fingers were one thing we didn't share. She must have seen it too. When crazy butterfly net guy was out of twig-crunching earshot, Jane jumped from behind the tree and leaped back on the path.

"A dead bird. He had a dead bird in his net," Jane squealed.

"I know, right?"

"This is a bird sanctuary. He can't bring his giant lynx cat in here to kill birds. I've brought injured birds here to be fixed up and released back into the wild."

Random, injured animals found Jane.

"There are by-laws, even real laws, maybe, probably, legislation against that kind of thing," she said.

Look out, kilt-wearing bird-scooping guy – there was no stopping Jane now from trying to save the bird kingdom.

"There's got to be an international convention for the protection of birds. We have to save the birds. We should tell Mom."

That's Jane – she's all about the rules and the blabbing.

"What are you, a bird lawyer all of a sudden? We're not going to tell Mom. Telling Mom didn't help in our last mystery. Forget about the rules. The bad guys always do."

Jane's face fell, deflated. Dial back on the sarcasm, I reminded myself. I put my arm around her shoulder and steered her to where we left our bikes.

"A guy killing birds in a bird sanctuary. Something is going on." Jane brushed the dirt off her hands.

I'd been beak to beak with too many dead birds lately, but I smelled a mystery as well. We slogged through the heavy bush until we got back to the bike path. We tried to keep out of trouble. But trouble seemed to have us on speed dial.

Chapter Three
Bird Killer of Another Kind

Blog post title: *Yin: 1, backyard song bird population: -1.*

I posted the adventures of Yin the Ferocious Bird Killer on our blog. Jane surfed the web for a bird killer of another kind, the Scottish bird killer, like it would be right there on his website:

ScottishBirdKillerandgiantlynxcat.com.

We were in our bedroom. We both had our own laptops and we had a dog now. Lucky was at my feet and inched a chewed and saliva-covered tennis ball toward me. We were allowed to stay on our own more now. Our parents thought a dog would keep us busy for the summer. Yeah, that and the volunteering Mom said we had to sign up for.

Jane was the queen of the search engines, so if any-one could find him it would be her. I tossed Lucky her tennis ball. Too many animals, and they all gravitated toward me instead of my animal-loving sister. Sure, I loved animals, but I loved books more; they don't drool on you, and you don't have to throw them a ten-nis ball a hundred times a minute.

Jane emerged from cyberspace. "Here's an article, from the local newspaper, about birds."

"Good, we can post it on our blog beside the Yin story, as a link to information about birds and the en-vironment." We usually tried to find something about animals in the rainforest. That seemed more exotic, somehow. "Or maybe do a blog post about the cat by-law here. You know, how your neighbor can kidnap your cat if it's wandering around in their yard. The cat goes to lock-up, has its day in court and you have to pay a hundred bucks to get it out."

"I'm not talking about our stupid blog or the by-law. I'm talking about the bird killer."

"Ohhhhh, twin on a mission. Back away from the scary Jane," I said.

"Listen, you wanted a mystery. Well, nothing is more mysterious than what we saw today," Jane glow-ered.

"Okay, already." Clearly, I had touched Jane's ani-mal-loving nerve. "What does it say?"

She read off the site. " 'The songbird population is down in some places as much as 70 per cent.' That's incredible."

"Hey, you sound like Mom and Dad with all those statistics. Next you'll want to conduct an experiment." I scratched Yin on the head; she was leaning against me, sleeping. "Way to contribute to the declining songbird population."

"Be serious for just one moment of your life, Cyd."

"Twin freakout – proceed with caution," I shot back. "Well, you can't blame Yin for that. She only killed one bird." Yin was now on my lap, in the curled up *I'm-going-to-be-here-for-a-while* pose. Lucky, tongue lolling out, was giving me the emerald-eyed jealousy stare. Her ball lay out of arm's reach until she rolled it closer. I grabbed the wet tennis ball and threw it – ugh, foiled again by the animal kingdom.

"I'm not blaming her. This is not about her. What is the link between the songbird population and the Scottish guy with a butterfly net?" asked Jane. She scratched her chin in a classic girl detective pose, considered the clues, and then scrolled down.

"Does it say why the songbird population is down?"

"The usual suspects, habitat change, and urban sprawl – you know, new houses being built – and growing cities, blah, blah, blah," she read deeper into the article. "It all decreases the number of insects. Birds need insects to live."

"Whoa, that's where I draw the line, no more mysteries that involve insects. I'm still scratching those mosquito bites from the last mystery." Not really – that was last year – but the memory made me itch.

"This is similar to the last mystery, but different. Fewer frogs meant more mosquitoes. Birds are doing us a favor when they eat bugs. If this guy gets rid of all the birds, the world will be overrun with creepy crawly bugs eating anything that's leafy and green."

"I'm all for using the literary device of exaggeration in my writing, but don't you think you're laying it on a little buggy? Save the world from an invasion of army ants – sounds like a science fiction movie."

"Okay, maybe the whole world won't be overrun – but our city will be." Jane's head was out of sci-fi land and back in cyberspace.

"That's good stuff for the blog – maybe a close-up picture of an army ant eating through the jungle," I said.

My thigh had gone numb from the weight of Yin the amazing bird killer turned lap cat. We called her Yin because half of her face was white, with a black circle around her eye, and half was black. Her body was a combination of black and white patches. We came up with the name when we were five, but later found out that Yin and Yang are opposites within a whole – kinda like Jane and me. We were identical twins, but in some ways we were exact opposites.

"Hold on a cyber second. None of this has anything to do with the crazy guy with the net." She slammed down the lid of the laptop and stared at me like I'd know the answer, just because I was the two-minutes-older twin.

Pressure was on. I tried to avert Jane blowing a gasket. She had a long simmering fuse, but when she blew – look out. I scratched Yin under the chin. "What would a cat do?" I mused, listening to her purr. "Go to where the birds are. That's it, we'll go to where the birds are."

I jumped up and Yin sprawled onto the floor. She squawked. She was none too happy with me. "Cat treats for you later, Yin." I swiveled toward Jane. "Mom wants us to volunteer. So we'll volunteer at the Wildwood Bird Sanctuary."

We were twelve years old. Too old for day camps and too young for jobs. Just the right age for mysteries.

"That's brilliant." Jane flipped open the laptop. The search engine whirled as her fingers went crazy across the keyboard. "Wildwood Bird Sanctuary. Here it is."

I perched on the bed and peered over her shoulder at the screen. The mug of the Scottish butterfly net guy popped up on the screen.

"Ahhh!" We both sprang back like he was right there in the room. "Why is he on the site?" I said.

" 'Aviary Finch, Director of the Wildwood Bird Sanctuary,'" read Jane.

"Wait a minute, an aviary – isn't that a bird cage?"

Jane opened a new tab in the browser and typed the word "aviary" into the dictionary site. " 'An aviary is a large enclosed area. Birds fly free in it and it is often filled with vegetation resembling the wild.' " She plugged in another word and announced, "and 'a finch is a songbird with colorful plumage.' You're right on, Cyd, or should I say 'write on'?" Jane mimicked typing just to make sure I got the joke.

That was as far as Jane's funny bone extended. But she was right; a mystery was brewing like Dad's steeped tea.

"So a guy named giant-birdcage-songbird is the director of the bird sanctuary." I held my chin in my best girl detective pose.

"I'll click on his bio." Jane read on, " 'The esteemed Mr. Finch joins the Wildwood Bird Sanctuary from his home in the glens of Scotland, where he managed the famous 'Toad in a Hole' Bird Sanctuary. Seeking greener fields... ' "

"More like dryer fields here," I interrupted. "The only place dryer than our city is the dark side of the moon."

" 'Seeking greener fields,' " Jane repeated, " 'Aviary Finch brings his unique style of bird care to the sanctuary.' "

"I'll say it's unique. Killing birds would be frowned on in most bird sanctuaries."

" 'Aviary is an avid fan of Shakespeare, especially Shakespeare's play *Macbeth*.' " Jane scrolled down. "It says he's joined by his wife Cygnet Finch, and they live in the cottage on the Wildwood Bird Sanctuary land." Jane turned to me.

"Both of them have bird names." I peered at his photo. His eyes were red-rimmed and his nose ended in a point like a beak; it was also rimmed in red. His terracotta-colored hair was done up in a crazy scientist haircut, and a fuzzy cattail of a moustache completed the look. His hair was a shade less red than mine, but my hair didn't look like that dude's. His photo appeared beside a link to a site on the birds of Scotland, and he looked surprisingly like the red-legged partridge.

I jumped off the bed and paced the room. "Cygnet, Aviary, red-legged partridge, songbird decline." Lucky thought I was playing with her and kept rolling the tennis ball at my feet. "None of it makes sense. Why kill birds if your job is to keep them safe?"

"Why indeed?" Jane said in her detective voice. She was one step ahead of me, her face buried back in the computer screen. The printer roared to life and two sheets shot out. Jane grabbed them, took one, and shoved the other one at me. "Volunteer sign-up forms."

"Let's go all Nancy Drew on this mystery," I said, "but first I need a pen."

Jane was already halfway through her form.

I pried a pen from Yin's mouth. It was covered in cat saliva and teeth marks. I spied what Jane scribbled for the answer to the first question:

Question 1) Why do you want to volunteer at the Wildwood Bird Sanctuary?

Answer 1) To save the birds.

I spread the form before me on the desk and filled it out.

Question 1) Why do you want to volunteer at the Wildwood Bird Sanctuary?

Answer 1) To get my sleuth on!

Chapter Four
Bird, Meet Nerd

" 'Climate change, mining, forest industry, more pesticides used by farmers … ' " Jane read off the laptop screen.

"Is that your grocery list?" I joked that my twin had a dweeb gene, but with scientists as parents we had to work extra hard not to be thought of as science nerds.

"Research; have to be prepared," replied Jane.

Sure, we were smart in school; who wasn't these days what with the Internet and all? – wait a minute, I sounded like one of my parents there.

Mom signed our volunteer forms with glee. It involved volunteering, science, and we happened to mention that it might form the plot of the next mystery we'd post on our blog. I don't think she heard that part; all she heard was "keeping us out of trouble during the day." With lunch packed and the dog walked, we hopped on our bikes and sped to the sanctuary. It's not like we didn't know the way. We knew the bike paths in this town like Lucky had a brain map to all the bones she buried.

We skidded our bikes to a halt in front of the sanctuary cottage. Jane locked both bikes to the fence. I pressed the bell on the cottage door and waited, rubbing my sweaty palms together. Nothing. No foot shuffling or handle-turning noises. Jane joined me. I pressed the bell in and held it, just in case it didn't ring the first time.

"Hello, twins. So we meet again."

The door was still closed, but the voice was behind me. We swung around. A sweaty teenager stood before us.

"Jane and Cyd, right?"

"Todd. From the Safari Sleepover at the zoo last year." Jane smiled.

"At your service, my ladies." Todd doffed his baseball cap and bowed low before us.

Jane giggled.

I gave my head a shake. A little bit of Todd stretched on for miles. Todd had come between a snake, the Cheese Pie Man, and us in the first mystery. So, I guess I should have been grateful.

"Hey Todd. What's up?"

"Volunteer coordinator extraordinaire." He pointed to his nametag that didn't say any of that. It just said *Todd*.

Todd had a water bottle slung across this chest like a rifle. He was dressed in khakis like he would be bushwhacking through the Amazon jungle, not hiking through the bird sanctuary in our small city.

"With school out, I'm working here for the summer. It's a big step up from the job at the zoo." Todd pulled out the key ring that was on a cord attached to his belt and let it snap back in. He groaned as it hit his side. "Tons more responsibility. Hey, how's your mom? Remember I took a class at mini-university from her. Both your parents are esteemed."

If esteemed meant full of hot air, this guy was esteemed, all right. He was like the science nerd older brother we didn't have but our parents would love to adopt. I wondered if he was an orphan.

"She's fine, Todd. We're looking for Aviary Finch. We start volunteering today."

"This is the Finchs' private residence. You were supposed to meet me at the bird sanctuary visitors' center."

I stepped forward. "If by private residence you mean 'house,' yeah, we get that. We still want to meet the big guy. We've got a few questions." Jane pulled at my T-shirt.

"Cyd, we'll have to be more subtle if we want to get behind the scenes at the sanctuary," Jane whispered in my ear. "He's not the enemy." She threw Todd a grin.

Subtlety wasn't my best font, but she was right. We were here to volunteer. We needed this bird nerd to get us into the inner workings of the sanctuary.

I stepped forward and clamped hands with Todd. "Where did you want us to volunteer? We're interested in all aspects of bird life."

"Maybe in the office, where we can see Mr. Finch in action. We hear he's quite, ah, *esteemed*," said Jane.

"I was thinking in the bird hospital..." He walked down the path to the visitors centre and motioned us to follow "... we can start you in the pigeon wing."

"Bird hospital," I whined when out of earshot. "What do pigeon poop, smelly birds and broken beaks have in common?"

"Stop fussing. Put your mystery writer face on and observe everything."

"They can all be found in the bird hospital."

Jane wasn't listening. She puppy-dogged after the bird nerd like Lucky when I had a forgotten dog treat in my pocket. Her backpack swayed back and forth from the weight of her mystery detective notebook.

Sunlight seeped through the trees that formed a canopy over the dirt path. In the background I heard construction noises – must be from downtown.

The visitor center was a round building and lined with floor-to-ceiling windows. One window was open and the center acted as a giant aviary; birds flew in and out. We walked past a group of day camp kids on our way to the offices of the bird sanctuary.

Bird nerd was ahead of us. Jane and I stopped dead in our tracks – like that dead bird through the cat door – when we saw him.

"Girls, I'd like to introduce you to … "

"Aviary Finch, Scottish bird expert." Jane extended her hand.

Bird killer, I wanted to add, but didn't.

"We read your bio online. We're interested in knowing more about you. Maybe we could shadow you for a day," said Jane.

Jane was right. This was our chance to clip the wings of this mystery even if it meant shoveling bird poop, or shoveling compliments.

"Oh, aye, of course lassies, always happy to talk to fledglings about my passion," Aviary said. An owl clutched Aviary's upheld arm, which was in a large thick glove. "Meet Mr. Hootenanny – he's a Scottish Barn Owl that I brought over from the homeland. Trained him myself."

It was a magnificent bird. Beautiful heart-shaped face draped in soft, delicate-looking feathers. Jane and I held back – that owl's beak looked like a can opener and I guessed it was as sharp as one.

On command Mr. Hootenanny hopped off Aviary's arm and on to a perch. Aviary snapped a bird handcuff – er, clawcuff – around the bird's ankle and on to the wooden perch.

He turned back to face us.

"Can you teach me?" Jane asked. She held her arm up and motioned to the owl.

"Not so fast. Do you have a gauntlet certified by the International Owl Training Society of Scotland?"

"I can scare up an old oven mitt," said Jane.

"That should do, bring it with you next time." Finch scratched behind Mr. Hootenanny's ears, or where I imagined his ears were beneath all those feathers. "I trained him from an owlet. He broke a wing in a farming accident. I used to chew up sausages, spit them out and feed him like his mother would have." Finch pantomimed a demonstration.

That was altogether too much information. This didn't seem like the same Finch we spied in the woods.

Jane joined Finch and approached Mr. Hootenanny. She inched her arm out slowly, and the hoot rubbed his head against her hand like Yin would.

"I taught him how to hunt," Finch said as he sized up how good Jane was with Mr. Hootenanny. "Yes, it is time to train someone else to care for wild animals." Finch gazed at Mr. Hootenanny and I think I saw the light reflect off tears in his eyes. "Maybe even release my dear owl into the sanctuary."

He looked away, then leaned back and watched the birds fly in and out of the sanctuary. "I can blether on for hours about birds. I love birds, everything about them," Aviary Finch said.

Right then, as if to put in large caps what he was saying, a bird flew into the office from the visitor center. Finch grabbed it in his claw, I mean hand, and held it to his face.

"Oh, my sweet," he cooed, making papa bird chirps as he coddled the bird in his hands.

I shot a glance at Jane. "Creepy," I mouthed.

"So many birds, so many birds … " he repeated but the tone changed from love to disappointment.

It looked like he was squeezing tighter. "Too many birds... always chirping, chirping, chirping."

The bird nerd, Jane, and I exchanged a glance.

"How about I take that." Todd pried Finch's fingers from the bird.

Finch woke, as if out of a dream, and was startled by what he was doing. "Yes, must not grip so hard," he murmured.

"We'll take that to the bird hospital," Todd pointed his chin toward the door leading out of the office and into the hospital, "… give it the once-over. It will be your first patient, girls." He forced a smile to cover the worry on his face.

"That dude's gone cuckoo," I said as I followed Todd and Jane to the bird hospital.

"He's just under a little stress. I keep my eye on him just to make sure things are all right," said Todd.

I didn't think Todd had heard me, but he was obviously worried. He stroked the baby bird's feathers and made sure nothing was broken. Jane and I looked at each other. Was a madman running the bird sanctuary?

Chapter Five
Bird Hospital

As glamorous as it sounds, after four hours of cleaning out birdcages, I was done. Jane, on the other hand, was assisting Todd in a delicate procedure of setting a pigeon's wing. Seems this pigeon was found on the edge of the sanctuary where he most likely flew beak-first into a skyscraper. Every pigeon in the pigeon wing of the hospital seemed to have a broken wing.

Members of the ancient Jain religion believe in not killing any living creature. That's Jain, not Jane; my sister doesn't have her own religion. Most of the members of the Jain religion live in India. Some even carry a brush when they walk to sweep away the insects so they don't step on any. I'm thinking they'd never worked in a bird hospital.

We packed up our backpacks and Todd went into the storeroom to get more tiny splints for broken bird legs.

"It's not going to work, Finch. There are too many birds."

Jane and I perked up when we heard a gravelly voice coming from the office. It was a voice we hadn't heard before.

"Souris, I have a plan." Finch protested.

"I've seen your plan. It consists of a butterfly net and a cat as fat as an upholstered couch cushion."

Jane and I bee-lined it to hide behind the door, which was open a crack.

"Who's Souris? – souris is French for mouse," said Jane.

"Thanks for the French lesson brainiac, just listen will ya? We might find out why he's killing birds," I said.

Jane slumped behind me. "It could be a clue, ya know, a play on words," she said.

We couldn't see Souris from where he was standing in the office. We could only see Finch.

"But it's working, Souris. I got one yesterday. One down, three thousand to go …" Finch's voice trailed off as if his mind was taking flight around the aviary.

"That's the problem Aviary, it will take too long, one cat-eating-bird at a time. That's not enough of a plan."

Finch sighed and held his face in his hands.

"We need more cats," said Souris. "And fewer birds. Running a bird hospital isn't helping our problem. We agreed. We have to get rid of the birds to make way for the cranes."

" '... they say, blood will have blood.' *Macbeth*, Act III, scene iv." Finch murmured under his breath as he looked around to see if they were overheard.

"More cats," I whispered.

"Fewer birds," Jane echoed.

"What are you doing at the door girls? Did a bird get out?" Todd stopped dead and assumed the bird-search position, which consisted of splaying out his arms and looking down at his feet to make sure he hadn't stepped on any escaping birds.

Jane and I stood up. "No, nothing," I stammered brushing my palms against my shorts like I had dirt on my hands. "Who's the dude with the mouse name?"

"Monsieur Souris Vole. He's French and runs some big international real estate conglomerate. He's a patron of the environment."

"Todd, I know teenagers like to show off, but you're using a lot of big words here."

"His company builds condominium complexes all over the world, and word around the birdseed tray is that he likes the outdoors," Todd explained in slow-motion words like we were twelve-year-olds. Hey, we *were* twelve-year-olds.

Jane pulled out her notebook. "What does he want with Finch?" She fished around in her backpack for her pen, clomped her molars down on the cap, pulled it off and spit it to the ground. She held her pen poised to take notes. She was on fire – girl-detective-wise.

"Probably fundraising. The sanctuary is always looking for donors. Look, I just got my permit to drive a moped, now that I'm fourteen. And I can drive a car if I have an adult with me and a ... car. Anyway, I could drive one of you home on my moped ... Jane?"

"That's great Todd, but we've got our bikes. Maybe next time." Bird nerd had a mode of transportation slightly faster than a bike. That was good to know: it might come in handy in solving this mystery.

I spotted Vole and Finch exit the office and leave through the sanctuary. I grabbed Jane by the arm and tugged her toward the door. I motioned with my head that we should exit stage left, and she caught my drift. She slipped me my backpack, and we navigated through the groups of school kids in the sanctuary before Todd could show off his learner's permit picture to us.

A few short sprints once we were outside, and we caught up with Finch and Vole on the path. They headed toward the cottage where our bikes were parked. We only saw Vole from behind as his short, stubby legs carried him forward. His bottom swayed from side to side and his body pitched forward as he walked. Finch trundled by his side on his bird-skinny legs. They both stopped dead on the trail. We dived under the nearest bush, and we were close enough to listen to their conversation.

"Aviary, I can see it now." Vole swept his arms out and looked around like he was a king surveying his kingdom. "Not a bird in sight and the only green you will see will be in your bank account." Vole had a slim smile on his mug.

"Spread the birds out all over the land." Finch copied the arm sweeping motion. "I just want the noise to stop. I want to live in my cottage in peace."

A bird-chirping symphony could be heard on the warm breeze that brushed my face.

We trailed them to the cottage where Finch bade Vole good-bye with an awkward bow and salute. Vole made his way to the end of the trail and hopped into his black car with shaded windows.

" 'There's daggers in men's smiles.' Act II, scene iii," mumbled Finch.

I squinted through the sunlight to see the license plate, being the ace detective that I am. All I could see were dollar signs – $$ – in green. The engine noise screeched through the air like an eagle cry and the car sped away. I heard a noise at my feet and looked down. A small rodent-like creature scurried back into the woods. At the same time, a red-legged partridge flew past me from one tree to another tree on the other side of the path, toward the cottage.

"What were they talking about? Even if they wanted to, they couldn't get rid of the birds and the trees. This is a protected site."

For once Jane's fascination with the rules paid off. She was right.

"So, why get rid of the birds? It doesn't make sense," I said.

"And what was that about daggers and smiles?" Jane asked.

I shrugged.

We hopped on our bikes and pedaled home. First day on our volunteer job and we were stuck in a mystery like a bird claw in mud.

Chapter Six
That Rodent Vole

"Souris Vole." I paced back and forth in a classic detective-thinking move. Lucky, close on my heels, thought I was playing a game. "Souris – French for mouse. We already figured that out. Voler – is a French verb for 'to fly.' Mouse Fly: that doesn't work."

The search engines groaned trying to keep up with Jane as she pounded in clues. "Wait a minute, Cyd. Vole – this time it's not French. I think I have it." She read something off the screen: "A vole is a small rodent, it looks like a mouse but has a stouter body, a shorter hairy tail, a slightly rounder head, and smaller ears and eyes."

I swung Jane's chair around so she was facing me. "Are you kidding me? Souris Vole, his name is Mouse Mouse?"

"No joke."

She broke out of my grasp, swiveled the chair back, and read on. Clearly, she didn't grasp the significance of this most awesome nickname. "Mouse Mouse," I grinned. "That's the best nickname ever."

"Let's see, they are related to lemmings and musk-rats. Owls, hawks and cats are their predators, and they like to eat nuts." She leaned over and scratched Yin behind the ears. "Are you going to catch a vole next time, you ferocious jungle cat?"

Not interested in the baby cat-talk, I resumed pacing. Mouse Mouse indeed.

Jane spun back to the laptop and splayed her fingers over the keyboard. "Finch can't 'spread the birds out' either. Many of the birds at the sanctuary are migratory and they come back there year after year. They need that habitat. I'll slap his name into the search engine and see what pops up."

"You don't want to disturb an animal in their habitat. Just try to move Yin off her spot on my bed and whoosh, open paw, claws out, smack across my hands. Isn't that right, Yin?" I gave her a cuddle.

Jane's eyeball rolling and engine searching was interrupted by Dad.

"Girls! Dinner."

He was barbequing his famous ribs. Well, they were actually Camembert Oulette's, or as we liked to call him, Cheese Omelette's, famous rib recipe. The only place Omelette was cooking was in the prison kitchen, because he had whisked up the giant frog caper. Dad missed the first mystery when he was in England for work. He was home this summer, but Mom had a big experiment simmering in a flask up at the university, so we wouldn't see much of her.

We tumbled down the stairs, Lucky in tow, still deep in the mystery of the man with two names.

"Four orders of vanilla-basted ribs ready to be gnawed on. Gnash your teeth into one of these."

I fake-laughed. While Mom was bookish scientist, Dad was pure science nerd. He even had the glasses to prove it. He also thought he was funny, and we humored him, so to speak. His apron said *Dinner's ready when the smoke alarm goes off.* He was a good cook, though, and we fell on those ribs like a pack of hungry wolves.

"How was your first day of volunteering?" Mom said between chews, sauce dribbling down her chin.

"Let me get that for you honey." Dad leaned over and wiped it with his napkin. Mom winked.

Gross.

"I cured a bird." Jane said. "It had a broken wing and I fixed it."

I was going to add that I had shoveled more bird droppings than the guy who cleaned out the elephant cage at the zoo, but I remembered that we didn't talk like that at the table.

"I got some help from a kid named Todd. He's the volunteer coordinator and he took a class from you, Mom, at mini-university," Jane added.

"Hmmm, Todd. Doesn't ring a bell." Mom said and shoved roasted potatoes down her gullet.

"We met the owner of the bird sanctuary," I blurted out like Lucky trying to get some attention; all eyes had been on Jane. "Aviary Finch – means giant-bird-cage-song-bird." I grinned and waited to be told how clever I was. But no.

"That reminds me." Dad licked his fingers, then wiped them on a napkin and pushed away from the table. "An invitation. It was in my mailbox at work from the Dean – the Dean is the head of the department," Dad explained. "Seems there's a function at the bird sanctuary that the Dean wanted us to attend. It's a reception for a prominent businessman who donated money to the sanctuary." Dad went to get the invitation.

"What's his name?" Jane and I blurted out, mouths full.

"Girls, finish chewing before you talk. This isn't the hippo enclosure at the zoo."

Dad came back in the kitchen with the invitation. "Souris Vole. Huh, never heard of him." Dad lobbed the invitation down on the table.

I snatched it up and smeared the card with barbe-cue sauce. Jane and I locked eyes on the invite. "How come you got invited?"

"Local scientists being in touch with the commu-nity, community outreach, that kind of stuff. Maybe if he's interested in environmental issues he'll want to donate money to the university. You girls want to come with us? Then we can see your new volunteer gig."

"Sure," we said at the same time.

The invitation was our ticket to spy on Souris Vole. Dad was in a band, so he used words like gig. Sounds cooler than it is. He was in a Renaissance band and played the lute. Which meant we went to a Shake-speare play in England last summer when we visited him on sabbatical. That was the best nap I ever had. Dad gave me his copy of *Macbeth* when we got back and I'd been thumbing through it to see if I could fig-ure out the language. It was like a mystery written in Elizabethan code.

"I bet Todd was invited, since he works there," Jane added.

"Then he can meet you two," I said.

"Why not? Sounds groovy," replied Dad.

Jane and I locked eyes and smiled. Why not, in-deed? Todd was our ticket to infiltrating the sanctuary, and the invite was our ticket to digging Mouse Mouse out of his hole. I attacked my ribs. Lucky was at my feet. She looked up, tongue lolling to the side. Lucky needed an apron that said, *Any food that falls on the floor is mine.*

"Speaking of friends, you remember Mrs. Katze down the street?" asked Mom.

"*Friend!* That *wrinkly* was no friend of mine."

"Cynthia, we don't refer to senior citizens as wrinklies," Mom said.

"Yeah, they like to be called oldsters," Jane added.

"Not really, Jane," Mom said.

"Remember when Lucky's ball ended up in her yard and Mrs. Krusty Katze said it was her ball now? She was crustier than an old loaf of French bread. She could turn white cheese blue." I was on a roll, a French roll.

"Anyway, she moved into an old folks home today," Mom said.

"Oh." I regretted my earlier outburst.

"I thought as part of your volunteering this summer you could go visit her in the home."

"What? Volunteering? More like *volun-told*. The bird sanctuary is one thing, but an old folks' home? Who am I, Mother Teresa of Calcutta with a dab of Mahatma Gandhi thrown in?"

"Cynthia, that's more than enough." Mom's raised eyebrows peeked out from behind her straight brown bangs.

"Let her go, Mom. When she's on a tear, there's nothing stopping her. Best to let her run out of steam."

"All old people do is talk about the olden days before everything was invented, like gum. They would just chew on a stick or something before that. And the Internet. Don't even get me started. It's bad enough we have to explain technology to you two, but the most sophisticated technology she had was the gramophone and I'm not even sure what that was." I ran out of steam.

"Well, if you're done, Cynthia." Mom put her fork down, crossed her arms, and gave me the look – the mom look. "What I was going to tell you was that her family had to give her cat to the shelter because she isn't allowed to take it into the home with her. I thought you and your sister could take Lucky over to the home and visit with her. It would brighten her day.

"But she loved that cat," I blurted out.

"It's a big transition, moving into an old folks' home. I arranged it with the lodge; they said they'd love to have you girls and Lucky visit." She picked up her fork, speared another potato, and glared at me. "Are you up for that, Mahatma?"

That was my mom's idea of sarcasm. Not bad under the circumstances. I wish there was an undo button on my mouth so I could take back what I said. "They took her cat. That's gotta hurt."

"Don't old folks' homes allow pets?" asked Jane. "Pets are part of the family."

"They let them visit," Dad explained, "but not live there. I talked to her grown-up children and they were devastated to have to take her cat away."

Just then, I felt Lucky's cold tongue lick my bare foot. I felt a twinge in my heart for Mrs. Krusty Katze.

"First thing in the morning, we'll visit her," Jane said.

I nodded, and the next rib kinda stuck in my craw.

Chapter Seven
Back in My Day, Dear ...

"She's trying to kill me. It's a complicated plot ... " I shouted into the wind. We rolled to the old folks' home on our bikes.

"Yin is not trying to kill you." Jane pedaled ahead of me, and Lucky trailed her.

"Her paw pressed firmly on my windpipe at four in the morning! Okay, it's not that complicated, but what would you call that if it's not an attempt on my life?"

"She's trying to wake you up to play with you. Cats are nocturnal. You know that."

I knew that, all right, every night when Yin chewed on my chin to wake me. Dogs were diurnal like humans. At least they let you sleep through the night.

I coasted up to the entrance of the old folks' home and braked beside Jane. She'd already locked her bike to the railing; I threw mine on the ground beside hers.

"Aren't you going to lock your bike?" she asked.

"Who's going to steal my bike at an old folks' home? An old grandpa guy with a new hip?" Lucky jumped on me and licked my legs. She was a perfect old-folks'-home-visiting dog.

We strode to the front desk. Jane got there first. "Our mother signed us up for the 'visit a senior with your pet' program."

"We're here to see Mrs. Krusty … er, I mean Mrs. Katze," I added.

"Why, there you girls are. I've been waiting for you." Mrs. Katze said as she walked toward us from the lobby. She had a big smile on her face.

"Hello, Mrs. Katze," Jane and I said, in unison, while Lucky jumped up to try to get her attention.

"It's Kathleen, but you can call me Kitty."

"Kitty Katze," I whispered to Jane under my breath.

"Not now, Cyd."

"But that's a great nickname. Kitty Katze!"

Kitty was stooped over and about as tall as Jane and me, which is to say short for an adult. Her white hair was cut in a bob and she had a caved-in jaw. She wore a sweater even though it was summer. The sweater was covered with cat images.

She was halfway down the hall with Lucky, headed to her room. Lucky would be the easiest dog to kidnap. She'd go with anyone. We followed and passed by the open doors of the other seniors' rooms. The rooms were small. The TVs were on and the volume was turned up loud. Most of the seniors were sitting in chairs or lying on their beds. "Jane, this isn't right. How come no one is visiting these people?"

"Most people are too busy, you know, work, Internet ..." Jane and Lucky ducked into Kitty's room.

"But they are somebody's grandma or grandpa or aunty or uncle. They could be outside in the yard at least, getting a little sunshine on their bones." It made me think of my grandma in England. We hadn't seen her since last year. The smell of fish coming from the cafeteria made me think of some of the food we'd tasted there. Some great and some nasty.

I turned into Kitty's room and stopped dead. We'd never been inside her house, but it looked like she had jammed her life's possessions into this one room. Her room was filled with pictures of cats, stuffed cat toys, ceramic cat figurines, and cat fridge magnets. She strolled Jane through the cat-filled memories of her life.

"Here's my sweet Contessa Cuddles." She stroked the picture like she was petting the cat. "I was a real pistol in the cat-show world, up until a few years ago. Can't get around much now." Her eyes turned sad like a dark cloud covering the sun. She stopped herself before there was a cloud-burst of tears. She shoved the picture at Jane and continued the tour of the tiny space stuffed with the artifacts of her life.

"Back in my day, Contessa was a Supreme Grand Champion. We'd go from cat show to cat show and she'd win all the ribbons." Kitty's sunken-in jaw turned up with a smile at the memory. She pointed out each prize and recounted the stories of how Contessa Cuddles cat-clawed her way to the podium for the ribbon. Finally, she sat down in an enormous pale-green armchair that looked like it had swallowed her. Lucky leapt on her lap and made herself comfortable. Kitty looked happy, yet sad, if that's possible.

Not to be outdone by Lucky, I handed Kitty the brownies Mom had made. The first one disappeared into her sunken-in jaw as she dentured it. She took the other one, wrapped it back up, and stored it in a drawer beside the chair like there was going to be a brownie drought.

While Jane and Kitty were talking cats, I took Lucky with me and rallied the other seniors to go out in the garden. Those who could walk, hobbled out with their canes and sat in the sun. I pushed a couple of seniors who were in wheelchairs. Lucky greeted each of them. I don't know who loved the attention more, the seniors or Lucky. I heard stories about the olden days, which may come in handy as a writer. They asked me about what types of things I liked to do. Some of them even knew about e-mail and the Internet. When lunch was called and the seniors moved into the dinning room, I went back to retrieve Jane.

"Kitty and I are going to enter Yin in the cat show in a couple of days," Jane said. Kitty was sitting in her big armchair looking like Yin after she caught a bird.

"That's a great idea. It might thwart her attempts on my life."

"Kitty is going to help me get her ready and give me tips about showing Yin and everything."

"And we're going to spring Contessa Cuddles out of the animal lock-up," Kitty added.

I slid Jane the famous sideways glare. "What? That's crazy."

Jane elbowed me in the ribs. That was twin-speak for *zip it*. I changed my tune.

"That's great. But where's she going to live? I thought she wasn't allowed to stay at the home."

"Jane said she could live at your house and she'd bring Contessa here to visit me."

I handed Jane the *are you crazy?* glare on a platter. "I think we'll have to talk to our parents about that first."

Kitty's face deflated like a soufflé. Sure, the two-minutes older twin gets to break the old lady's heart.

Jane said quickly, "I'm sure we can work something out with our parents. Maybe we can get Contessa out to enter her in the cat show." Kitty perked up at this. She scratched Lucky behind the ears and smiled. Funny, when we left, she didn't look like cranky Mrs. Krusty Katze anymore, she just looked like Kitty.

"You can't make promises like that to an old lady. She'll be crushed if we can't get Mom and Dad to agree to take Contessa."

Jane unlocked her bike. "Come on, Cyd, you saw that place, she's dying in there. She needs her cat. And I aim to get it back for her." Jane slammed her bike helmet on her head, jumped on her bike, and headed home. Lucky trailed behind.

You didn't have to be Mother Teresa or Mahatma Gandhi to feel for those old folks. We'd get that cat back if it was the last thing we did. And knowing Mom's rule about no more pets, it might just be.

Future blog post title: *Kranky Krusty Katze begone!*

Chapter Eight
Do You Want Nuts with That?

Mom and Dad arrived home at the same time we did. Dad's "How was your day?" was ignored as Jane hip-checked him to get into the house and up the stairs.

"We've only got time for a quick bite to eat before we need to leave for the reception at the bird sanctuary," Mom said as I raced Jane up the stairs. I knew Jane had a plan.

By the time I got in the room, Jane was on the bed and the laptop whirled into action. Jane let out a yelp. "You're not going to believe this."

"What is it?"

"Contessa Cuddles has been adopted."

"Already? By who?" I asked.

Jane scrolled down the webpage of all the cats. Contessa's photo had a banner across it that said *on her way to a new home*. Jane clicked on it. "It says 'Contessa is off to her new home with Aviary and Cygnet Finch.' "

"What the … ?"

"More cats, remember? Vole said he needed more cats and fewer birds. They've enlisted Contessa into the bird-killing air force."

"It would be more like the army, get it, the birds would be the air force … army instead of air force."

"Cyd, you don't get it. Contessa Cuddles was a show cat. She ate shredded shrimp out of a champagne glass. She slept in a cat-bed lined with velvet, and wore a fake diamond-studded collar. She won't last a day out in the wild of the bird sanctuary. We have to get her back to Kitty."

"Girls, it's time to go," Mom called.

"Let's get our Nancy Drew on," I said. "Grab your notebook – we're on detective duty tonight, Jane. We need to find that cat and find out what Finch and Vole are up to." I shoved my digital camera into my backpack, also my copy of *Macbeth*, and hurled myself down the stairs.

We picked up Todd on the way. He gushed when he met our parents.

"I'd love to come and watch your experiment," he said to my mom. Maybe he had a crush on her – gross. "I've been following your careers."

"My parents have more degrees than a thermometer," said Jane.

He laughed a little too loud and a little too long. Jane grinned; I sighed. This could get tiring really soon. We needed to put him to work.

The reception was in the large visitors' center. It looked more like an aviary than it had a couple of days ago. Large birdcages with exotic birds had been brought in, along with a few more tropical plants. A brightly-colored parachute was strung up from one corner of the ceiling to the other corner. It looked like a giant hammock. A string hung down from the middle. I didn't remember seeing that before.

"Cyd, tropical plants ... remember?"

I had a flashback to the tropical plants in our last mystery. That's where they kept the giant frogs, in the tropical plant green house at the university. I shivered, then caught myself. "Shake it off, Jane. Focus on this mystery. Our goal tonight is to find out what's going on with Finch and Vole, and Contessa Cuddles."

"With everyone busy here, let's snoop around and see if we can find Contessa." Jane grabbed pieces of salami and cheese and motioned with them. "Just in case we find her."

We did the walking backward thing right into the office area. No one noticed. "Hello?" I shouted into the offices. No response. Jane followed me into the animal hospital. No one there either.

"We're alone," I said.

"Get your sleuth on," Jane responded.

"Hey, that's my line," I cried after Jane as she headed for Finch's office.

"What do we do first?" I asked when I caught up with her.

"Find Contessa Cuddles and then figure out what's up with Finch and Vole," Jane said.

At the mention of her name, there was a little meow.

"Did you hear that, Jane?"

Jane was on the floor, calling out Contessa Cuddles's name and making friendly cat noises. She held out the salami and cheese. Contessa emerged from behind the filing cabinet. Jane picked her up.

"You are every bit as majestic as Kitty said you were." Contessa purred and chowed down on the food. She was safe with Jane.

"A cat trapped in a bird sanctuary, and she's hungry?" I said.

"Maybe Finch is keeping her as a pet and not releasing her to kill birds in the sanctuary?" Jane added.

"Forget about surviving in the wild. She couldn't survive in a bird hospital where half the birds had broken wings," I said.

Contessa finished off the salami and licked Jane's fingers. She hunkered down into Jane's arms like she was going to be there for a while.

"I don't know what we should do with her, but Jane, we've found Contessa. Let's get back out there and figure out what's up with Finch and Vole."

"You're right, Cyd." Jane put Contessa down and stroked her one last time. "She's fine for now. Let's split up. I'll tail Finch and you lay out some crumbs for that mouse, Vole."

"Good turn of phrase, that'll come in handy when we write up this mystery." Jane led the way back to the reception.

"And what about the bird nerd?" I asked. He was in the corner where he bird-dogged our parents.

"He's fine where he is for now," she said.

"You're getting a little bossy, Jane."

She threw me a withering look. "My sleuthing skills are slickening – and you're jealous."

"Don't get me wrong, I like it, and nice alliteration, by the way."

"Let's focus on the mystery – if we let these two have their way all the birds will be gone and the town will be overrun with creepy-crawling leaf chewers."

I headed for the cheese platter in search of Vole. His thin smile went from ear to ear. His small beady eyes were peering into the large bowl of nuts. His hand combed through them and emerged with a fistful. He opened his fist and picked out the nuts one by one. From his hand to his mouth, he ate in a continuous stream. He was startled when he noticed me, and nearly choked.

"Cyd," I held out my hand. Vole extended his hand like a paw and shook it. Salt from the nuts coated my hand.

"Would you care for some nuts? They are very good. I asked for them especially. Peanuts, cashews, walnuts, almonds, Brazil nuts … and seeds. Sunflower seeds, pumpkin seeds, sesame seeds…."

Those aren't the only nuts, I thought. "I'm a new volunteer in the animal hospital," I interrupted. Sometimes adults get distracted and don't know when to stop talking. I didn't need a list of the nuts of the world. I glanced from him to Finch; there were two of the world's finest nuts right here. Vole was back at the nut bowl. He had a plate with a cracker and sprinkled nuts on it, then put another cracker on top. He made a nut sandwich with crackers. He *was* crackers.

"Would you like some nuts with that?"

Vole looked at me as if it was the first time he'd seen me. Maybe his tiny ears couldn't hear me.

"So what's your interest in the animal sanctuary? Do you like birds?" That was as good an opening as any. Mom always said I needed to learn how to make small talk, chitchat.

Vole was back to picking through the nuts and seeds in his hand. He looked at me, distracted. "Yes, I like birds, would like them more someplace else." He shot a glance at me.

Move over, small talk – hello, bluntness. "What does that mean?"

"Birds … lovely … I want them all over the place for everyone to enjoy," he backtracked. He leaned in and scratched close to my eye with his, claw – uh, fingernail. "Stay away from Finch, leave the birds to me or I'll gnaw you like fresh tree bark."

I jumped back and grabbed his hand. A few adults turned, startled by the commotion.

"Just brushing some salt off her cheek, I'm a messy eater." Vole's laugh was evil/jokey, like sour jujubes – sweet, yet with a bite.

I flipped his hand away from me and he went right back to digging through the nuts. Did that just happen? I searched for Jane. Finch called everyone's attention to the front. He prepared to make an announcement. Todd rushed up to us.

"Monsieur Vole, Mr. Finch asked me to bring you up to the podium." Vole allowed himself to be led away, but not before handing me the plate with his nut-and-cracker sandwich.

"Got nuts? Yeah, I've got a whole room full of them." I said to no one in particular. A bird landed on my shoulder, hopped to the plate, and started picking at the seeds. "Great, now the whole bird kingdom likes me too." I put the plate, with bird, on the table and made my way to the front so I could hear the speech. Jane had saved me a spot.

"Great. Speeches. Why do adults always think people want to hear them make a speech?"

"Did you get any intel?" she whispered.

"Here's some intel: Vole threatened me with his claw. 'Stay away from the birds,' " I imitated. "Vole's a nut, and I don't mean the everyday, garden-variety, quirky kinda nut. I mean a full-fledged crunchy, yet chewy, lightly salted and roasted nut."

People milled around and waited for the speeches to start. Vole scurried up the stairs.

"That's it? That's all you've got – that he's a nut? Well, let's update the blog because that's big news, Cyd."

"Wait a minute, I hardly had five minutes with the mouse. Are you taking sarcasm lessons by the way? Because that was a nice one."

"Ladies and gentlemen, volunteers and distinguished guests ... " Finch intoned from his speech as a bird touched down on his shoulder. "It is my distinct pleasure to introduce to you tonight, Monsieur Souris Vole… pause for applause," he said as he looked up. The blank faces of the audience gazed at him. He realized that he wasn't supposed to read that part out loud. His feathers were flustered now. He stared at the crowd a little too long, and then went back to his speech. "He's an international real estate developer, mogul person, which means he builds buildings and he's hoping to do some business in our lovely city."

Jane and I giggled. I pulled the camera out; this was getting good. The adults tried not to laugh.

Vole shuffled to the microphone and Todd lowered it to a height that the slouched-over Vole could reach. When he spoke into the mic, his voice sounded like nuts being ground between his teeth.

"Yes, I'm here tonight to announce a donation I'm making to the bird sanctuary. Tonight I will give the bird sanctuary a thousand …"

"Dollars!" I gasped.

" … a thousand pounds …" he continued.

"Must be pounds sterling, you know, British money," said Jane.

" … a thousand pounds of birdseed. Cast your eyes to the ceiling."

Jane and I were in the middle of the floor. The adults started to move to the sides and were murmuring the adult equivalent of *What's up?* I pointed the camera to the ceiling.

"There's one of our volunteers. Cyd, I believe, could you do the honors and pull the string?"

"Hey, he remembered my name. Finally, I'm getting a little attention around here. Jane, a chair please."

Jane dragged a chair over for me.

I stood on it and reached for the string. I gave it a big yank and the brightly colored parachute ripped opened in the middle like a piñata. Birdseed cascaded over me like I was standing under Niagara Falls. I managed one click of the digital before I was completely covered and spitting mad. I swiveled around, birdseed flying off me in all directions, and I caught the shocked look on people's faces.

Vole was beaming and Finch looked befuddled. The crescendo of clapping commenced – you know, when it starts with one clap and builds up to the whole room clapping. I scrambled down and shook the last of the birdseed out of my ears. I spied around for my parents, located them and hopped over the birdseed toward them. Jane, ankle-deep in the stuff, slogged through the birdseed like it was slushy snow.

"Was that dramatic enough?" asked Finch.

"Yes, as dramatic as that Shakespeare chap you drone on about. Now we proceed with the tragic part." Vole lowered his voice then raised it again. "But let's get this cleaned up! It will be distributed far and wide in the city so birds can enjoy it far outside the trees of the bird sanctuary."

Jane and I swapped knowing glances.

"So that's what he's up to," said Jane. "He's trying to get the birds out of the sanctuary. But why?"

"Strange way to go about it, dumping a lifetime's supply of bird food in a bird sanctuary. How bird-brained is that? He's more confused than a bowl of mixed nuts. This is going to be a tough case to crack." I'm still funny even when covered in birdseed and humiliation.

Chapter Nine
Cat Show Mania

Blog post title: *Birdbrain, Meet Birdseed!*

It was the next day and I, for one, still had birdseed lodged in a few interesting crevices, like the bend in my arm and my belly button. It was worse than a day at the beach. I wanted to get back to the bird sanctuary to see what happened with all that birdseed, but we'd promised Kitty we'd find her cat and we had to report back.

A handful of Kitty's senior citizen friends waited in the lobby. They gushed over Lucky. I handed a grandpa-type guy the leash and he led Lucky and the others into the courtyard. Lucky would be fine for a while.

We trailed Kitty to her room.

"Did you find Contessa Cuddles?"

"We did," I said.

"Oh, my dears." She took my face in her hands, so happy I thought she was going to cry.

I looked at Jane; she shrugged. Oh, great, I get to break an old woman's heart.

"You'd better sit down for this, Kitty. It's good news and bad news."

Kitty's face registered worry. "Is Contessa all right?"

I took her arm to help lower her into the giant armchair. "We found Contessa and she's fine."

"Is she at your house?" Kitty had more questions than a pop quiz. I took it one step at a time.

"She's not at our house, and she's not at the animal shelter anymore. We couldn't adopt her because she was already adopted."

Kitty's spirits sank along with her body as the chair swallowed her up.

"But she's been adopted by a nice couple, Aviary and Cygnet Finch. They run the bird sanctuary."

"Oh, no! Contessa's *afraid* of birds." Kitty wrung her hands like she was wringing out a swimsuit.

"Well, the good news is that they're keeping her in the office and at their cottage as their pet. It's in the bird sanctuary, but no birds will get her."

Kitty thought on this for a moment.

I was thinking, too. A cat afraid of birds – for now. I hoped Finch wouldn't recruit Contessa into his fiendish feline army of bird killers.

Kitty kneaded the bottom of her sweater. "If she can't be with me, then that is the next best place for her."

"Cyd and I volunteer at the bird sanctuary, and maybe they'll let us take Contessa to the cat show," Jane said.

Kitty perked up.

I glared at Jane. "We can't make promises to Kitty that we can't keep," I whispered under my breath.

We promised Kitty we'd be back tomorrow to take her to the cat show. We searched for Lucky in the court-yard of the seniors' lodge. Lucky was cuddled up in the lap of an older gentleman.

A dog treat convinced Lucky to leave the lodge. She'd never had so much attention and, by the looks on the faces of the residents, they didn't want to part with her. The mystery at the bird sanctuary and the avalanche of birdseed would have to wait. We had a cat show to prepare for.

****

Stuffing a cat into its cat carrier is a life-changing ex-perience, for both the cat and their human. Yin trans-formed herself from a curled up ball of fur to a flat, limbs-spread-out, paws-stretched-to-the limit, claws-at-their-ready maniac. Shoving her into that cage was a two-twin job. Jane clamped one hand on each side of the cage, to hold it still, and I tried every which way to push Yin into it.

It was extra life-altering for me because I now had a lot less blood flowing through my veins. Instead, it flowed freely over the hardwood floor.

I'd been smart enough, however, to wear a long-sleeve shirt, which was now covered in cat hair. Loud squawks emitted from the carrier, but Yin was in.

Cygnet Finch had agreed to let us take Contessa Cuddles for the day and enter her in the cat show. In fact, Cygnet was going to visit us there. The logistics were like solving a mystery. Dad was driving Yin and us to the bird sanctuary to pick up Contessa; then it was over to the seniors' lodge to pick up Kitty; then it was a drop-off-of-all-cat-lovers at the cat show for the day. Jane had a small suitcase full of cat food, human lunch and snack food, cat toys, camera and notebook.

We arrived at the community hall as they were setting up for the cat show. Kitty insisted that we get there early to decorate our cage. Rows of tables filled the hall. A number of cat cages were on each table.

Since Kitty, a.k.a. The Pistol, was back, the organizers elected her the Grand Show Ring Manager for the day. Kitty was thrilled and pulled a bright yellow T-shirt over her sweater. It had *I'm the Cat's Meow* emblazoned across it in letters that looked like cat tails with a few paws thrown in. Kitty rustled through her bag of cat supplies and plucked out a whistle on a long string. "Just in case," she said, as she put it around her neck.

"There must be two hundred cats in here." The cat-erwauling pierced my eardrums.

"Close. There are one hundred twenty-three," Jane read from the program.

I could barely hear her. The sheer howling sounded like hundreds of crying babies.

We found our cages; Contessa's was next to Yin's. Jane set up the cage with her bed, food, and water. Yin ditched the cat carrier and slid into the cage, where she collapsed on her cat bed.

"Oh, sure, she's happy to get out of her carrier and into the cage," I said as Yin lapsed into a deep sleep.

"What's the matter with her?" Jane asked.

"Looks like she's in a kitty coma."

Jane poked Contessa to wake her up.

"Don't sweat it, Sis. Would you rather she pitched a feline frenzy on the judges and scratched them? That would get her kicked out of the cat show faster than cat-food breath."

"There you go, my sweet Contessa," Kitty was in a world of her own, petting her cat. "It's just like before, Contessa. You're back with me now."

Jane and I exchanged worried glances. They were only back together for one day, and then it was back to the lodge for Kitty and back to the Finchs' for Contessa.

Jane and I strolled around the community hall; she had her pen poised and notebook in hand. "It's like being in another culture," she said.

"More like the planet of cat-crazed people, in the galaxy of cat litter boxes, far, far away, that we didn't know existed," I added, in my best science-fiction movie voice.

The place buzzed with activity. Purebred cats were combed, puffed up, and readied for their debut in the ring. Owners frantically shook cat toys in front of their cats, begging them to be alert. Cat wranglers rushed felines from ring to ring.

Jane and I stared at a cage that was like a two-floor cat apartment complete with a hammock, and a kitty couch for lounging. It was decorated in a tropical theme. "That's way over the top by two-thirds. Yin wouldn't even like something that fancy," I said.

"Yeah, Yin is happy with your lap, getting a whiff of fresh air, and pouncing on the grass."

We wandered back to Kitty. She had Contessa on her lap and was brushing her.

"You know what to do, Contessa. When the judge picks you up, purr. There's a good kitty," she slipped her cat a treat.

There was a hairless cat beside me that looked like an extraterrestrial when she wrinkled her forehead. Note to self: stop watching the UFO channel. "Those hairless cats freak me out more than the tail-less ones," I said, as I surveyed the hall.

I scoped out the activity and tried not to be mowed down as people rushed down the aisles, past cages, to the six judging rings at the front of the hall.

Yin was up for her first judge. Jane dragged her from her cage and Yin's body flopped in her arms.

"Now that's passive resistance, Yin style." I followed Jane as she put her on the judge's table.

The judge was an older man with a mustache. He wore a brightly colored paisley sweater and had just flown in from Italy. Kitty, Jane, and I settled into the chairs in front of the ring and waited for the judge. Jane squeezed my knee nervously.

He stroked Yin. "Oh, she is so beautiful, *magnifico*." He held her up in front of his face and stretched out her body. "Her coat has such an unusual pattern."

Jane squealed when he gave her a Best in Color ribbon. She squeezed my knee even harder when he gave Yin fourth place. Kitty beamed.

"I know we like Yin and think she's great, but who knew she was so special?"

"I *told* you, Cyd."

We went with Kitty and Contessa to a couple of show rings. Contessa swept the ribbons in both. She was a Supreme Grand Master after all, so that wasn't a surprise.

Later in the afternoon, Cygnet Finch arrived. We'd met her when we picked up Contessa, so it was easy to spot her in the crowd. She was petite and thin, like a sparrow. Wisps of her gray hair fell out of her bun and framed her face. We flagged her down and she made her way through the lanes of cat cages until she got to us.

"Are you alone?" Jane asked.

"What's that, dear?" Cygnet cupped her hand to her ear.

"*Are you alone,*" Jane repeated.

"Am I on the phone? No, dear," she said, patting Jane on the shoulder. "I'm here in real life. I'm not on the phone."

Jane shrugged, scooped up her cat, and we headed for the ring. Only one more show ring for Yin. She hunkered down on the judging table and we waited for the judge to start.

Then the head of the cat fanciers bustled in and grabbed the mic.

"We have the distinct pleasure today to introduce two new guest judges. One is a naturalist and a long-time lover of animals. The other is a patron of animal sanctuaries the world over."

"Don't tell me it's Finch and Vole," Jane whispered.

Chapter Ten
Cat Show Clampdown

I didn't have to tell her.

" … I present to you, Aviary Finch and Souris Vole!" The judge led the applause. Clearly, Cygnet was not alone.

"What are they doing here?" Jane asked.

Finch hobbled out from behind a curtain. Vole shuffled into the hall, his hands covered in salt from a recent feast of nuts.

Jane held Yin down on the judging table and I was on the other side of it. I heard Vole command Finch:

"You know what to do, Finch?"

"As Lady Macbeth said: 'Look like the innocent flower, but be the serpent under it.' Act I, scene v,'" Finch intoned.

Vole mumbled something and gave his head a shake as he was escorted to another ring. Finch stayed in the ring Yin was showing in.

"Those two add up to trouble," I said.

"Evil times two." Jane glanced up at the table where Yin was cowering under Finch's bony fingers.

"Ye are a fantabulous feline." Finch stroked Yin from her head to the tip of her tail. "First place," he declared.

There was a gasp and the room fell silent.

Sure, Yin was cute, but she wasn't a showstopper.

"I must examine this cat in-depth, behind the scenes." He put Yin back in her show ring cage and placed it on the floor.

"That's highly unusual." Kitty said a little too loudly and everyone looked at her.

"No way I'm leaving Yin there." Jane scooted up and grabbed Yin.

"I'll take her back, Jane, and you stay with Kitty." I took Yin back to her own cage, and I returned in time for the next cat to be judged.

A giant orange tabby was placed on the table amidst whispers. I heard the words "improper procedure" sneered more than once. People in this crowd had no idea how improper Finch could be. An image of him brandishing a butterfly net next to his giant tailless cat flashed through my mind.

"A fine lad," Finch looked in his ears and stroked his coat. "First place," he declared.

Another gasp, but this time the room didn't fall silent. It buzzed like a beehive. Finch stuffed the cat back in the show ring cage and placed it on the floor close to the curtains separating the show ring from the back of the community hall.

Kitty heaved herself out of the chair whistle in hand. "He's flipped his wig."

That was old-lady trash talk for, *He's crazy on a stick right side up.*

Not only did Finch not know the difference between a Supreme Grand Master and an alley cat, he wasn't so hot at math. There couldn't be two first places. He was giving away ribbons to everyone. He kept placing the cages on the ground.

Four more first places were declared. Kitty sprang into action.

"That drip must be stopped. I don't care if he's punch drunk on catnip!"

Kitty hobbled to the judge's table and stood beside Finch. She blew her whistle right in his ear. She looked madder than a wasp.

"Ahhh, the birds! Stop the noise!" Finch cried.

Kitty swiped the mic out of his hand. "Thank you, Aviary Finch, for participating in today's celebrity judging. It's the first – and last – in a series of promotional events to bring more attention to the cat show."

She glared at Finch. "Yes, bow, smile and nod your head." Finch obeyed. "There you go," and she grabbed his arm and ushered him out of the ring.

Jane and I took that as our cue and followed.

Kitty's phony smile merged into a sneer when they were away from the crowd. "You're done like dinner, Finch. Now we'll have to re-judge all of those cats. How about you and your mouse friend make like a banana and split?"

Kitty's old spunk was back. It reminded me of when she lived on our street.

Finch and Vole skulked around by the back of the hall for a while and then they vamoosed.

"Attention everyone: there are some cats missing." The head of the cat fanciers' voice echoed through the hall over the loud speakers. "Total lockdown, lockdown of your cats." There was a mad rush as people at the show ring grabbed their cats and zoomed for the cages.

I had put Yin back in her cage a while ago; we were with Kitty watching Contessa get judged. We gathered her and Kitty up, and headed back to the cage. Many cages were empty. But Contessa was safe.

The cat owners were catatonic. The wailing of the cats had stopped, but the cat owners were caterwauling for their beloved pets.

"Finch and Vole are to blame for this. I don't know how, but I have a sneaking suspicion that they are behind it." I secured the latch on Contessa's cage.

Kitty trundled back to the show rings and blew her whistle like crazy.

"Cyd, Yin's missing."

I swung around to face Yin's cage. It was empty. Her cat paw blanket was strewn about the cage. Water had splattered on the bottom of the cage and food was scattered everywhere. They must have grabbed her and run.

I put my arm around Jane. She shrugged it off and wiped her eyes with the back of her hand.

Jane slammed her fist on the cage. "Now it's personal."

Chapter Eleven
All-Cats Bulletin

Blog post title: *Police issue an ACB – All-Cats Bulletin – for the cat-nappers.*

A quick text to Dad got us out of there. The police had checked through the building and around the area in case the cats were wandering around, but it was clear that they had been taken away from the community center. Many of the cats had still been in their cages when they were stolen. We had a pretty good idea of where that location was, but the police didn't want to listen to kids.

We'd already planned to drive Kitty home, and since Finch and Vole were nowhere to be seen, we drove Cygnet home as well.

"Those two lamebrains aren't going to get away with this cock-eyed caper. I didn't just fall off the turnip truck, you know," steamed Kitty.

I checked out how Cygnet reacted to the trash talk about her husband. She hummed to herself, so I guessed she hadn't heard. Contessa was in her cat carrier in the front seat with Dad.

"My connections in the cat community are as deep as a scratch from Yin."

At the mention of Yin's name, Jane whimpered.

Kitty held Jane's hand in her old, bony one. "Don't worry, my dear, I'll find Yin if it's the last thing they let me do before lights-out in the lodge." Kitty clenched her jaw with determination. It looked more sunken in than ever.

Jane was strung tighter than catgut on a guitar. Oops, better not mention *catgut*. Cat intestines were never used for guitar strings and tennis racquets – it was mostly cow gut and they don't even use that any-more. How did I know that? It didn't matter now. The point was, Jane was wound tighter than my hair, when I tried to style it around a brush.

A pamphlet fell out of Kitty's bag and onto the car seat as Dad helped her out the door.

I picked it up. "*Soar like an Eagle in your High Rise Condo. Ideal for Seniors,*" I read out loud. "Kitty, this is yours." I handed it to her.

"You keep it. It's just another ploy to get seniors out of the way. They'll tear down the last of the old cottages on the edge of the sanctuary, where some seniors still live."

Dad took her arm and walked her into the seniors' lodge.

"Moving us here and there, like we're old suitcases. Stick us in a high-rise so no one can see us. I'm going to get Contessa back ... " Kitty's voice faded in the breeze.

I stuffed the pamphlet into my backpack. We had bigger issues now than the emancipation of old people. Dad got back in the car and we headed to the bird sanctuary to drop off Contessa and Cygnet Finch.

Jane leapt from the car and stormed into the cottage. "Where is she? Where is my cat?" Every nerve ending in Jane's body was on fire.

Dad and I were right behind her. He lugged the cage with Contessa.

"Jane wait, you can't barge into their house," Dad said.

Cygnet shuffled up the rear. "Dear, there be no one home."

By this point Jane was in the kitchen scouting around for her cat.

Cygnet flipped up the breadbox and grabbed her hearing aid. "Yin isn't here, why would you think that?" She fumbled to get the device into her ear.

"They've got my cat, and I want her back." Jane stood with her hands on her hips. The Stonehenge of twins.

"The police are on it now," Dad said in his don't-make-any-sudden-moves voice. He placed the cat carrier on the floor and let out Contessa. She felined it to Jane and rubbed against her legs. Jane gathered up Contessa, buried her face in the cat's fur and made sobbing noises.

Holy hairball, Batman! I thought it, but knew enough not to say it.

Jane pulled her face out of the fur and wiped away tears and cat hair with the back of her hand.

Cygnet put her hand on Jane's shoulder. "What's done is done – that's Shakespeare or something … Aviary does natter about him."

"Where are Finch and Vole?" Breaking away from Cygnet's attempts at comforting her, Jane channeled some of Kitty's spunk and old-fashioned language. "Those two are bonkers and they've got my cat."

"They're not here, my dear. They were at the cat show all day. Now they're out on bird sanctuary duty."

Cygnet used the don't-make-any-sudden-moves voice. "How about a nice scone with homemade jam and a spot of tea? That will make you feel better."

"I don't want to feel better." Jane plopped herself down on the couch and clamped her arms folded. "I want my cat." That was Jane's last word on the subject.

Contessa pounced up on Jane's knees and assumed a pose like an Egyptian cat. Jane quivered like lime-green Jello after Lucky had knocked a bowl of it on to the kitchen floor.

"The animal control officers are scouring the animal shelters and the river valley and everywhere else those cats might be." Dad eased down onto the couch and put his hand on her shoulder. "There were some mighty valuable show and breeding cats in that bunch, and their owners want them back."

"Are you saying Yin wasn't valuable because she's not a show cat?" Jane wrenched out of Dad's loose grip.

"Of course not. Yin's the most valuable cat on this planet and probably in the whole solar system," Dad said.

Nice save, Dad.

He nudged Contessa off Jane's lap and eased her off the couch. "In fact, Yin's priceless. You can't put a value on her." He inched Jane toward the door of the cottage and continued his nudging-Jane-out-of-the-cottage maneuver.

"They need the cats because of the birds," Jane ranted.

"Of course they do, honey," Dad said.

"They're trying to get rid of the birds one bird at a time," she continued.

"I'm sure it's just a misunderstanding," Dad said.

"One down, three thousand to go — that's what he said," Jane yelled back toward Cygnet.

"Sure he did, honey." Dad gave me the she's-your-twin-do-something-about-her look.

I shrugged.

"We don't blame the Finchs," Dad shouted back to Cygnet as we made it past the door and hit sunshine.

Dad tucked Jane and I into the car and he went back to talk to Cygnet.

Jane fumed beside me.

"There must have been another person involved. Someone snuck those cats from behind the curtain and from the cages when Finch and Vole were judging," I said.

"The songbird and the mouse work alone," Jane added in detective code.

"Where's Todd been all afternoon?" I asked.

"You leave him out of this. You've been on his case since the last mystery," Jane snapped.

"Don't be mad at me because your cat's missing."

"You were the last one who saw Yin. Maybe you're working behind the scenes with them."

Jane looked as shocked as I did. Neither of us believed she had just said that.

"Jane, are you kidding me with that? *Are you accusing me of being a double crosser?*"

"You never liked Yin. It's been one complaint after another: she's on your lap, she's making attempts on your life, she's coughing up hairballs – what's a little cat vomit in your shoe? Never killed anyone, did it? Maybe you left the cage unlatched for the thieves."

"That's crazy, Jane." My voice cracked. "How can you even *think* that?" I slouched down in my seat and turned to face the window. "I hooked the latch up. I'm sure of it. Besides anyone could have opened it."

Dad bid Cygnet farewell, but not before Cygnet shoved a bag of scones at him.

"These are for your girls. Some of my oh-so-tasty scones."

"Did she say anything more about the cat-nappers?" Jane asked.

"No. I'll take you girls home, and you can wait to hear from the police with Mom. Aviary and Souris are coming over for dinner tomorrow night and you can ask them if they have any clues."

Jane shot forward in her seat. "You bet I'll have questions for them tomorrow night." She sat back, grabbed a scone out of the bag and handed it to me. "I'm sorry," she whispered. I took the scone. It was as hard as a dog biscuit.

Mom was on the phone to the police when we got home. "No news, girls. The police think the thieves left the city with the show cats and dumped the rest. We could scour the riverbed for her. Where else could she be?"

"We need to put a picture of Yin on our blog."

Jane and I raced to our room. I nearly tripped over Lucky, who got tangled up in my legs as I bounded up the stairs.

"Where else indeed? What's your plan, Jane? I know you have one. I can hear the gears churning in your brain like the school hamster running on the wheel."

"No plan, I have no plan, Cyd. But I do know where Finch and Vole are."

The laptop whirled into action and Jane uploaded a photo of Yin onto the blog.

"We're going to tail them like Lucky at the dog park when she wants to play with the big dogs." Jane pounded her blog post on the keyboard: *Award-winning Cat Kidnapped!* "Here's the plan."

So, she *did* have a plan.

Chapter Twelve
Aye, Ye Wee Lassies

Beep...beep...beep... Todd steered the golf cart toward us on the narrow path. The attached wagon was filled to over-brimming with the birdseed from the other night. That seemed like a lifetime ago. None of that mattered since Yin had been kidnapped. Todd drove toward us but peered behind his shoulder to make sure the birdseed didn't spill out.

"Todd." I shouted and waved my arms like I was landing a plane. He couldn't hear me over the noise of the engine. The golf cart barreled down at us at a good two kilometers per hour. It wouldn't do much damage, but we still didn't want to be hit.

"You go left, I'll go right," I said to Jane mere moments before the cart was upon us. We dive-bombed into the brush.

Todd finally saw us. He was still glancing over his shoulder, and caught a glimpse of us when the cart passed.

"There you girls are. I never thought you'd show up. Well, let's not just lounge around in the bushes bird-watching all day. There's a lot of work to be done."

"We were almost mulch because of you." I stood up and brushed leaves and twigs off my shorts. I went to grab Jane but she'd bounced up, and her backpack, stuffed with snooping supplies, was already over her shoulder.

"I need you girls back at the visitor center. It's closed until we get that birdseed out."

"Todd, we've got bigger issues now. Yin, my cat, was stolen yesterday at the cat show, and Finch and Vole are involved."

"I can't help you with that. This is a bird sanctuary, not a cat-holding cell. I've got my own problems." Todd took off his hat and wiped his sweaty forehead. He looked like he could cry or scream.

Jane backed off the stolen-cat thing a bit. "What are you up to, Todd?"

"I'm taking this birdseed to a truck, and then it will be transported to a helicopter at the airport, which will fly over the city and sprinkle it over the parks and green spaces. I've been shoveling seed all morning."

"That's crazy," I said. A chorus of birds chirped, as if to agree with me.

"There's got to be a by-law against that," added Jane.

We now return to our regularly programmed Jane. It was nice to see my sister think about something, even momentarily, other than the missing Yin.

"Crazy or not, that's what I'm doing. There is a pecking order around here, y'know, and I'm pretty much at the bottom of the birdcage. I'm in a summer student job and I do what I'm told. We can't have that birdseed there forever."

"What do you want us to do Todd?" Jane approached him as if he were a dog that could bite.

"There's another wagon at the center and some shovels. Fill the wagon up and I'll be back for it." He started up the engine and trundled off.

We picked our way down the path over a trail of birdseed that fell off the wagon. "Todd's a little stressed out. Maybe we should bring him some of Mom's brownies. Like an employee appreciation thing," said Jane.

"So I'm Mother Teresa and you're a Girl Scout or something? First we need to find out what's going on with the songbird and the mouse. Get it? Those could be their blog character names."

"No, first we have to find Yin." Jane's steely determination returned. She stopped dead on the path and turned to face me. "Don't forget about Yin."

"How could I have forgotten about Yin? Especially when you blame me for her disappearance."

Jane held my gaze with her eyes. Her eyes blinked with tears or anger – I couldn't tell. She looked like she was going to say something, and then she turned on her heel and stormed up the path. Passive resistance, Jane style.

I followed at a bird-watcher's pace. I was worried. Unless Yin was in the Finchs' cottage, she wouldn't survive in the forest. Catching one bird didn't make her a wild animal; plus, there were coyotes at night. I kneeled down and scooped up a handful of birdseed. I let the birdseed slip through my fingers. Jane was way ahead of me.

The huge pile of birdseed was in the middle of the visitors' center where it had fallen the other night. The evening had ended right after the waterfall of birdseed. People had hobbled out over it, trying not to stumble, and digging birdseed out of their shoes.

Two shovels were stuck in the pile like they were waiting for us. The wagon stood empty nearby. Not a soul was around. A few birds pecked at the seed. Mr. Hootenanny, his feathers glowing in the shaft of light that shone through the skylight, was tethered to his perch. Jane inched over and held her hand out palm up. Mr. Hootenanny shuffled across the perch away from her. He wasn't as comfortable with Jane without Finch around.

"Jane, that's a wild animal, not a cat. It's not going to sniff your palm for treats."

"Finch is teaching me how to take care of Mr. Hootenanny," Jane added.

"Even Finch, crazy as he is, wears that giant oven mitt that covers his whole arm. Back off the bird and let's find out what's going on here." I headed toward the back part of the visitors' center. "Hello?" I shouted into the offices. No response. Jane followed me into the animal hospital. No one there, either.

"We're alone," I said.

"Get your sleuth on," Jane responded.

"Hey, that's my line," I cried after Jane as she headed for the office.

"Keep an eye and ear out for Yin, but let's rifle through his desk while we have the chance."

We'd lost any sort of shyness about snooping after our last mystery. But I kept one peeper on the door just in case. Was snooping wrong if it saved animals?

Finch's desk hogged most of the room in his office. It was a large antique wooden desk. Maybe he'd dragged it over from the Scottish Highlands, because it was twice as old and four times as dusty as any desk I'd seen. It was strewn with paper, and somehow the birdseed made it into his office as well.

There was the *Birds of Scotland* day calendar. It was open to the date a couple of nights ago with the entry: *avalanche of birdseed*. Yesterday's date: *Cat Show Caper*.

I flipped to today's date: *The plan proceeds – the noise stops!* was scrawled in dark, thick pencil lead. "Jane, look at this."

She stopped taking digital photos of the office and strode over. " 'The plan proceeds, the noise stops'? What does that mean? It's a bird sanctuary. There is no noise."

She picked up the calendar and started flipping through the pages for the next few days. That's when I saw it, under a pile of old-fashioned books, almost squished. The blueprints. I rolled them out. They covered nearly the whole desk. The blueprints lay flat on the desk, except for the bumps that were the stapler and other piles of paper.

"Here, look."

Jane swiveled to look. I held down the edges with my outstretched arms.

"Trees, and more trees. But not like the trees around here. These look like tropical trees, like in the rainforest. It's so dry here they can't grow tropical trees."

"Where is it supposed to be?" I asked. A cat rubbed against my leg. "Yin!" I looked down and it was Contessa. "Oh, carp." Relief and hope turned into fear and dread. I remembered why we were here. Where was Yin? Those two were up to something and it involved my sister's cat.

"But what about the quip Mouse Mouse made about money? How could they make money by planting a tropical garden?" I pondered.

"Maybe it would attract more visitors to the sanctuary," said Jane.

By this time, Contessa had jumped up on the desk and was trying to get under the blueprints like a kitten.

"Aye, ye wee lassies, what do we have here?" Finch's voice had an edge to it that we hadn't heard before. We froze in our sneakers.

"All this talk of money and by-laws; seems like ye be butting your brows in where they don't need to be." The voice was closer.

We swiveled on our heels and came face to face with Todd. He burst out laughing.

"Todd, you freaked me out. What are you doing here?" I asked.

"Just messing with you. Why aren't you shoveling seed?"

"We were on our way." I let the edge of the blueprint go and it snapped back up into a roll. Contessa slid behind the filing cabinet.

Todd bee-lined it for the door before we could. He braced his arm across the doorframe and blocked our way out. The smile erased from his face.

"No, really, what are you doing rifling through Mr. Finch's stuff?"

Chapter Thirteen
Crazy or Evil?

"We're all friends here, Todd." I inched toward the door.

"*Are* we, Cyd? Are we all friends?" Todd put his leg across the door as well, a full body block by a bird nerd. His eyes glazed over like he'd been staring at the sun.

"Todd, did you drink enough water today?" Jane yanked her water bottle out of the backpack and poured some into the cap. She handed it to Todd and he gulped it back.

Todd sighed long and low. His leg clumped to the floor; then he let his arm flop down to his side.

"Let's go sit in the shade, away from the visitor center. My mother packed us some salami sandwiches." Jane led Todd outside. He perked up at the mention of our mother.

After Todd had torn into and devoured the sandwich, I bottom-lined it for him.

"Look, are you crazy or evil, or do you just have sunstroke? We can deal with all three, but I think we prefer crazy to evil, unless it's sunstroke, that's easy to deal with. A little water, a hat …" Maybe *I* had sunstroke. I couldn't stop blabbing.

Jane said, "What my not-so-crazy sister is saying is that maybe you've noticed that there are some, ah, crazy, er, I mean, eccentric – uh, let's call them *interesting* happenings going on at the sanctuary. I don't know if you've heard, but we've quite a reputation for solving mysteries around this town."

"Yeah, yeah, giant frogs, scientist simmering in a flask, and the frog kingdom lives to croak another day. I scanned the blog," Todd said. "What do you want with Finch and the bird sanctuary?"

Jane handed him the water bottle. He took a long swig. Ugh, backwash.

"We need to know if you're involved in the goings-on with Finch and Vole or do you want to crack this mystery like a bird beak cracking open a Brazil nut?"

Todd took another swig of water. "That Finch is crazy on a stick right side up and I wouldn't leave him alone with a bird. And Vole, with his tiny mouse nose and the eating of the seeds, munch, munch, chomp, chomp. He's driving me nuts." Todd laughed at his own joke.

Seems he had run-on foot-in-mouth disease as well. Never mind. We could work with him.

He clawed at a spot in the dirt until there was a hole and shoved the water bottle in so it stood upright. "I'm in – those two are softer in the head than a goose-down pillow."

"What do you know so far?" I pulled out a sandwich. "We saw Finch and his giant lynx cat kill a bird."

"Vole's crazy for nuts and he's got more dough than a baking show, and by dough I mean money. Finch wants to get rid of the birds. Vole natters on about planting trees that grow nuts."

"But we need birds: they are like natural farmers. They increase tree growth by eating parasites and insects from bark, and they spread seeds from one area to another with their feet," said Jane.

"Can you get into the office?" I asked.

"Anytime, anyhow." Todd pulled on a string that was attached by a clasp to his pants pocket. Kinda like our parents' security pass to the university lab. On the end was an iron key that was probably smelt in the days of King Arthur. "Key to the visitor center and the key to that giant desk." He let the string snap back and it smacked him on the leg. "Ouch."

"Why would they trust you with that?"

"Finch wanders around muttering, and Vole shows up to talk about 'the plan.' Who do you think is running the center?

"Oh, right, so you're like the Bar-Headed Goose of Central Asia around here." How did I even know that?

Jane eyed me. "What are you talking about, Cyd?"

"It's the world's highest-flying bird. Todd's acting like he's the top bird in this giant feather nest of a bird sanctuary."

"Listen, I've got access. I'll help you, but I have one demand."

This should be good.

"I want some face time with your mom. She's a great scientist and she's all that and a side of test tubes."

"Okay, that doesn't even make sense, and gross."

"If I'm going to be a scientist, I need to start hanging with the big dogs in white coats, and not crazies like Finch with his butterfly net. Will you make it happen?"

Jane and I looked at each other. The silence was filled by the sound of bird chirps as the sun shone through the leaves of the trees. I motioned to Jane and we got up and walked away to talk about it.

"Maybe we don't need a sidekick with all his demands?"

"Okay, he sounds a little touched, but Nancy Drew had Ned," Jane said.

"Ned did whatever Nancy told him to do, but this guy wants to run the whole mystery. And he's got a crush on our mom, which is nasty."

"Let's be practical. He's got the keys and a car," Jane said.

"He's got a moped and a learners' permit to drive a car with an adult, and he's only two years older than we are. Besides, when are you practical?" I asked.

"You can't always be two minutes older than everyone. Sometimes we have to ask for help. If he double-crosses us, we'll say it was his idea and turn him in."

"Evil twin comes up with a good idea," I said, rubbing my hands together.

"Is he in or out?"

"He's in," I dragged Jane back to Todd.

Todd stood up as we approached.

"All right, bird nerd, here's how we're going to roll with this. You can come to dinner at our house and chat DNA theory with our mom. But you need to get us beak-to-beak with Finch. Deal?"

"Deal. Oh, yeah – I'm allergic to salami." Todd dropped to the ground with a thud.

Chapter Fourteen
Bird Nerd Blackmail

Todd looked dead. I grabbed the water bottle from Jane and splashed the rest of the water on his face. He popped up and swung his head around like Lucky after a bath. Water sprayed all over him and on me.

"Ahhhh, nobody's allergic to salami. I'm just messing with you. Stand-up comedy, if the whole science thing doesn't work out." He jumped up.

I planted both hands on his chest and shoved him back. "You scared the living birdseed out of us."

"Let's go. I'll secure the invite into Finch's cottage for lunch." He marched down the path.

"For a bird nerd he sure needs a lot of attention," I said. Jane smirked and we ran to catch up with him.

He halted in front of the Finchs' cottage and knocked on the wooden door.

"Todd, my wee lad, how lovely to see you again. Can you come in for some fresh granola with honey?" It was Cygnet Finch.

"Not today, Mrs. Finch, but I'd like to remind you that tomorrow we'll be here with Mr. Finch and Monsieur Vole for the staff and volunteer appreciation lunch."

"Oh, Aviary forgot to tell me, he's been so preoccupied recently. Yes, of course, and I'll make my famous beak soup."

"And these are Cyd and Jane, two of the newest volunteers," said Todd.

Two of the *only* volunteers, I thought.

Cygnet rolled her eyeballs over us like she hadn't just seen us yesterday. When she set her gaze on Jane she had a glimmer of recognition.

"What exactly are they preoccupied with?" Jane asked, but Cygnet didn't hear. Or else she pretended not to.

I extended my hand. "We met yesterday at the cat show, and the day before that when you agreed to let us take Contessa to the show."

"Yes, that cat business, messier than the litter box, I do say. Did your cat turn up yet, my dear?" she asked Jane.

"We're still looking. Have you seen her, Mrs. Finch?" Jane asked.

Contessa Cuddles tried to slip in the open door.

"Oh, ye wee heathen, how did you get out?" Cygnet picked up Contessa and stroked the cat. Contessa responded in kind by rubbing her face against Cygnet's and giving her a wet nose kiss. "Good thing she wasn't cat-napped yesterday. We just got her from the shelter. Lovely cat, isn't she?"

"She's a real show-stopper. You wouldn't want her to go missing," said Jane.

Cygnet closed the door.

"At least Contessa's not involved in the bird-killing escapade," sighed Jane.

"Okay, so that's done," Todd interrupted. "Get me an invite with your mom."

"Tonight? I was thinking later in the mystery, more like when it's solved," I said.

Todd was strolling down the path; he pulled the string with the keys and let it snap back. "Tonight, twins … or there might not be a mystery."

"I already regret this," I said.

I pulled my cell phone out and texted Mom and Dad at the same time: *friend 4 dinner 2night?*

By the time we followed Todd like the Pied Piper to the visitor center, we had a response from Dad: *awesome. B-B-Q'd ribs ok?! ;-).*

Dad tried way too hard to be cool. He was a good cook, but he only knew five recipes, though he did perfect them.

"All right, Todd, you're in," I yelled up the path to him.

"Tonight we have dinner with Todd, and tomorrow lunch with Todd, Finch and Vole. That's altogether too much Todd. What's wrong with this picture?" I asked.

"What's wrong is that we need to find Yin and get her back, and if it means having multiple meals with some shady characters then that's what we'll do," Jane said.

She was jumpier than Yin when she spotted a squirrel out the window. We caught up to Todd in the office of the visitor's center. "Crack open that desk, Todd. Let's see if we can make a detective out of you after all," I messed with him.

The size of the key was dwarfed by the desk. The key was tiny – smaller than my bike key.

He fiddled with it in the top drawer and it popped open. He made a great show of pulling it out like it weighed a hundred and ten pounds.

"Come on Todd, you're slower than a … "

"New World Vulture," interjected Jane.

I flashed her the *say what?* eye.

"What? I'm not allowed to do a little online research? Is that it, Cyd?"

Todd and I glared at her.

"Let's just say he's no peregrine falcon, the world's fastest bird," she added under her breath.

I elbowed him aside and took over. I gripped the bottom of the drawer. It was heavy. Felt like it was made of petrified wood. I pulled it most of the way out and held on so it wouldn't drop on my feet.

"Pencils! *Pencils,* Todd? This is what you blackmailed us for?"

"*Blackmail* is such an ugly word. I prefer mutually beneficial partnership. Maybe there's a clue here," he stammered.

Jane grabbed a handful. She examined them. "Here's a clue. Finch has chewed on each and every one of them." She shuffled through them one by one. "And it looks like he's got every pencil since grade one. Unless one of these pencils draws a straight line to my cat, they're useless." She raised her arm as if to slam the pencils down, then gently tossed them. Even in heartbreak she was a softie.

We needed to find Yin. I knew it wasn't my fault, but isn't the two-minutes older twin supposed to take care of the two-minutes younger twin?

I shuffled through the next few keys until I found one that would open a side drawer.

The drawer stuck when I pulled, but I managed to pry it open. It was full of gardening booklets. I pulled a pile of them out and Todd and Jane started flipping through them.

"*How to grow trees,*" Jane read the title. "Hundreds of them." Each booklet made a slapping sound as she threw them on the desk one after another. "Pecan, walnuts, almonds … maybe Vole talked him into growing nut trees instead of tropical trees."

"Birds love nuts," interjected Todd.

"Well, that wouldn't work; that would attract birds. Their plot is to get rid of them," I said.

"Fruit trees as well, apples, cherries, apricots…. Dad could make a nice cobbler, but that doesn't help us much," said Jane.

"Birds are allergic to apricot pits," said Todd.

Jane and I stopped and glared at him.

"Apricots are a member of the Prunus family and they create a bitter cyanide compound in the pit."

"Cyanide? I've watched enough horror movies to know that you can poison someone with cyanide," I said.

"In fact," Todd assumed a professorial tone – he would get along with our mom – "the pits and seeds of all of those fruits are like poison to birds."

Jane pulled out her notebook and scribbled away. Maybe Todd would come in handy, after all.

"It was in the staff training program. That's why there aren't any of those trees here now. You'd have to be as dim-witted as a dodo bird to plant those trees in a bird sanctuary."

"Unless you wanted to wipe out the entire bird population of the sanctuary like the dodo bird." Jane slammed her notebook shut.

"Apricots," I murmured. "It all makes sense now." I strummed my fingers against my chin.

Todd and Jane looked at each other, then at me.

"What makes sense?" asked Jane.

"Well, it doesn't really make sense. I just always wanted to say that."

We heard raised voices in the visitor center. It was Finch and Vole. They were close. We shoved the booklets back in the drawer. I heaved the drawer back into place just in time.

"Aye, what's all this chattering about?" Finch surveyed the room that included the three of us in a no-go zone. "And why are ye all in my office?"

Future blog post title: *Handy tips for girl detectives – how to slip out between a Finch and a Vole.*

Chapter Fifteen
Evil Times Two (E x 2)

"Dusting," I blurted out.

"Just cleaning up a bit," Jane echoed.

"Yes, sir. I thought I'd keep the volunteers busy while I shoveled the birdseed." Todd added.

I gave him a hearty sideways sneer, and a swift elbow to the ribcage. Finch might be the boss of us at the bird sanctuary, but we were the bosses of the mystery.

"We don't need any witnesses," sneered Vole.

Finch surveyed the scene. He wore the giant oven mitt and Mr. Hootenanny perched on his arm. A look of doubt crept over Finch's face. It vanished as quickly as an endangered species. "While that's all fine and dandy, but that's me done for today's work. Todd, lad, I need you to drive me and Vole to a meeting."

"At your service, sir," Todd saluted. "I've got my learner's permit and I practice driving, with my dad, in the parking lot of the grocery store after it's closed."

"Yes, yes, that's all well and fine. We're going to meet with some scientists."

Jane tensed up beside me.

I ripped off a piece of one of the booklets, scribbled our address on it, and gave it to Todd. He winked and mouthed *See you at dinner,* then trailed after Finch and Vole.

We headed home on our bikes. I wondered uneasily, "It couldn't be our parents they're going to meet, could it?"

"Nah, what are the chances...?" Jane's voice drifted into the wind.

We arrived home minutes before Todd showed up.

"Exciting news, girls," Dad beamed as he waved the barbeque tongs. "Your boss and his benefactor are coming over for dinner."

"Are you friends with Finch and Vole now?" I blurted out. Mom had a bad habit of inviting evil characters to the house – but Dad, too?

"What she means, Dad, is how did that happen?" Diplomatic twin to the rescue. "I thought you met Mr. Finch for the first time at the reception?"

"Yeah, you hardly know the dude, Dad," I felt compelled to add.

"Well, we got to talking and turns out he's a bit of an amateur botanist. Wanted to talk hybrids, and he didn't mean cars." Dad winked and waited for us to laugh at his joke. He carried on when there was no response. "Anyhow, he's trying to create a few bird-friendly species of trees in the sanctuary."

Jane's nails dug into my arm. That was painful twin code for meet in *Control Central*; that's what I called it. We bolted for the stairs. Jane called it *Nancy Drew's Hideout*. *Control Central* was, in fact, an enormous clothes closet built into our room. It was so big that we could climb up, using the shelves like a ladder, and sit on the top shelf. This is where we kept most of our spy toys. Like the invisible ink I bought from an ad in the back of a comic book. The ink wasn't invisible, but it was fun to think of how we could write that into one of our mysteries. We kept all our mystery novels up here and worked out our plots.

But we weren't sketching out a fictional plot twist now – it was the fate of the bird kingdom, and one cat that was at stake.

"They've got Dad involved." I gasped, out of air from running up the stairs.

"He's got to be able to figure out what they're doing. He's a scientist, after all. He must know those fruit seeds and pits would be poisonous to birds."

"Yes, but he's a friendly scientist and would give them the info, and then wouldn't know how they planned to use it," I added.

Mom called, "Girls, our guests are here!"

"And you can bet: 'what's a hybrid?' is going to be tonight's science-time dinner chat," I muttered.

We were good in science but we didn't brag about it because we picked up most of it around the dinner table. Like most famous writers, we just wanted to be left alone to write our mysteries and update our blog. We wanted Solitude Island, but the mysteries kept dragging us into Adventure Cove complete with a crew of crazies.

We clomped down the stairs to see Todd, followed closely by Finch and Vole.

"*Enchanté*, professor," Todd kissed our mother's hand while bowing.

"How sweet." Mom curtsied awkwardly in response.

"Yes, yes, that's all well and fine. Move along, boy," Finch chirped as Todd blocked the hallway with his theatrics. Finch lumbered under a basket full of apricots. He lobbed the basket into Dad's arms and Dad swayed under the weight of the fruit.

"Great, I'll throw some apricots on the stove and stew up a compote while we're eating, and we can have it over ice-cream," Dad headed for the kitchen.

Finch and Vole followed our parents into the kitchen and out on the back deck.

I leaned over the stair railing. "How about I get you a butter knife, Todd, so you can lay it on a little thicker?" Jane and I crept down the last few stairs and circled him like Yin stalked a bird.

"What's up with you and our mom, Todd? You're creeping me out," said Jane.

"I admire her work, is all." Todd picked at his fingernails and a kernel of birdseed flew out. "Besides, I need a better gig than babysitting Finch and Vole next summer if I want to get into university."

"Oh, you're ambitious, Todd, aren't you? Remember where ambition landed Macbeth." I mimicked a knife slicing across the throat.

Todd pulled a snake smile reminiscent of a previous culprit and slid into the kitchen.

"He's a four-alarm phony," Jane said.

"He's more plastic than spreadable cheese," I fumed. "But we need him – for now."

"Finch and Vole: evil times two." Said Jane.

"E squared," I agreed." We headed for the deck.

Dad passed the plate of ribs to Vole, who took one, clamped a fist on each end, and dived in. He tore the meat with his teeth and chewed like a hamster. Then he chomped from one end to the other like an old-fashioned printer going back and forth over the page.

He put the bone in his mouth and licked off the sauce. I half-expected him to crunch it and suck out the marrow like Lucky does. I glanced at Mom; she didn't even notice his appalling table manners.

Todd was busy filling up Mom's plate with food like he was an 18th century knight of the Volunteer Bird Sanctuary Corp. Jane watched Todd like a hawk as he fawned over Mom. Jane harrumphed in her chair with her arms crossed and shot Mom the emerald-eyed jealousy stare. Finch held a rib by the tips of his fingers, pinky fingers in the air, and pecked at it, pulling small bits of meat with each bite.

It was time to find out what these two were up to.

I glanced at Jane. She nodded, and I opened the proceedings with a question.

"Hybrids, eh?" Or maybe it was a statement. But it was out there now.

"Now a hybrid is ..." Dad began the evening's lesson.

"Sir, if I may ... ?" asked Todd.

"By all means," my mom said.

Jane and I were united in the rolling-back-of-the-eyes move. Todd – what a suck-up.

"If we're talking about plants, and I believe we are," he smiled at my mom. "A hybrid would be a creation of a new plant from two different species of a plant."

"That's me fed," declared Finch. He'd had one rib and a bit of salad. He hadn't touched his potatoes. Vole dug in the potatoes with a bone like he was looking for a grub.

"Are you sure you won't have more?" Mom passed him the plate of ribs, "There's plenty of food."

"No, my dear, I'll just have a peck of water, thanks."

Let's get this mystery back on track, I thought. "But why hybrids, and why now?"

"I want to feed my wee bird bairns. Baby birds love fruit, just like in my bonny Scotland."

I didn't understand half of what Finch said.

"That reminds me, Jane, owl training session to-morrow before the mid-day meal. Bring the longest, well-padded oven mitt ye have."

"Aviary asked me to experiment with two types of apricots, to make a super apricot for the birds." Dad took another rib.

"Why would he want to do that? Aren't there lots of things for the birds to eat in the sanctuary?" I asked. Jane's ears perked up like Lucky's.

Vole's dark eyes pierced me.

Dad didn't seem to hear because he was talking with his mouth full. Had everyone gone mad – table-manner-wise?

"Aviary, why don't you pop by the lab in a few days and we can see what we can come up with. In the meantime, I'll mix up those apricots into a nice crumble, saving a few, of course, for the experiment," Dad grinned.

"I can smell that compote. I'll clear the table and bring out dessert," Mom stood up.

"Let me help," Todd bounded up like a baby bird learning to fly, and was already clearing the table. Finch followed them inside. Jane, Vole and I stayed outside.

We were no further ahead in the mystery. I threw Lucky, the canine vacuum cleaner, a bone. I wished someone would throw us a bone of evidence so we could crack this mystery open and suck out the marrow.

Vole shot his hand across the table and sank his claws, er, nails, into my arm. I tried to pull back, but was trapped.

"It's best for you to get uninterested in birds. I wouldn't want to have to splice you and your nosy twin like a hybrid," he spat.

I yanked my hand back as Dad ambled onto the deck with the bowls and the compote; he was followed by Mom, with a carton of ice cream. Dad surveyed the scene. I clutched my arm, Vole sneered, and Jane sniveled. Dad did a brief double-take. He didn't say anything, but scooped up Souris Vole some ice-cream with a side of suspicion.

Chapter Sixteen
Fiendishly Feline

Jane pounded on the computer keyboard like she was busting out Beethoven's *Fifth*. "I'd like to roast that Todd like pumpkin seeds. 'Oh, can I help you with the dishes, professor?' " she mocked him.

"Hey, birds like pumpkin seeds." Now she'd dropped the mocking tone and was back to research-Jane tone.

"What are you talking about, Jane?" It was too early in the morning for sunstroke, and besides, we were in our room.

"I'm updating the blog. I'm making a list of seeds and fruits that birds like. Some birds eat insects and dead animals. It's fascinating."

"Yeah, positively spellbinding. Look, maybe we should back off this mystery." I rubbed my arm over the marks Vole's nails had left, "and focus on finding Yin. The owl training is a distraction."

Jane had got her fight back after last night. "Nancy Drew wouldn't let a brush with harm from a giant mouse keep her from finding her cat and solving the mystery. Not that she had a cat, but anyway. The owl training is a good chance for some alone time with Finch. So far we know … less than nothing."

She slammed down the lid of the laptop and swerved to face me. "Cyd, we don't have any more clues than when we first spotted bird nerd and crazy Scottish guy with giant lynx cat and butterfly net. Yin's still missing. Who knows if she's cowering behind a bush somewhere, or being held captive for Finch and Vole's plan? Finch should be dragged off in a net, instead of carrying one."

I slid the computer off her lap and flipped open the lid. I ran my eyes over the blog entry. *Bird Nerd and his plan for world domination, one compliment at a time.* Clearly, Jane had lost it.

"You can't write this. Todd will know it's about him."

"Someone has to stop him; he's a big phony. Oh, he's all interested in science all of a sudden and wants to hang out with our parents, and go to the lab. But he really wants a one-way ticket to a better job, so he can leave us on a perch at the bird sanctuary."

"Listen, Jane, Todd's not our problem. There's no point in being jealous of Todd."

"Jealous of Todd? Who are you saying is jealous of Todd? I can't stand the guy."

"I hate to misquote Shakespeare's *Hamlet*, but methinks the twin doth protest too much. Is everyone in my family in love with Todd?"

Jane pretended not to hear that and droned on with her rant. "Don't quote Shakespeare to me; you slept through that play last year. Now Todd's going to the lab with our parents and not even complaining about it, like he wants to hang out with them all the time." Her shoulders slumped.

I sat beside her and waited. She took a few deep breaths and exhaled all her anger at Todd. "Todd wormed his way into this mystery, now let's make the most of it. While he's making fish-eyes at Mom, we can hang with Dad and Finch as they create their hybrid plant. We'll be in the front seat on this mystery train."

I handed her the notebook. She scribbled and read out loud:

"Clue #1: Scottish dude with butterfly net killing birds;

Clue #2: need more cats and fewer birds;

Clue #3: Yin's kidnapped;

Clue #4: apricots; and,

Clue #5: we don't have a clue."

"We'll have more after lunch today at the Finchs'," I said.

I put up a new blog post title: *Twin misses cat as culprits create a hybrid of deception.*

Chapter Seventeen
Beak Soup

"Voice strong, point your finger, and bark the command word," Finch instructed. He had his full length gauntlet pulled up way past his elbow. Mr. Hootenanny was perched on Finch's arm ready for the command. "Mr. Hootenanny – mouse."

Hootenanny soared like an eagle, er, hawk, er, owl. He dove through the trees and straight for the brushes. He hopped out of the bushes with a mouse in his beak.

"Had to teach him how to hunt for himself." Hootenanny swallowed the mouse in one gulp.

"Here, you try it, Jane."

Jane had her arm in the brightly colored oven mitt. Aviary commanded Mr. Hootenanny to land on her arm.

"Mr. Hootenanny – mouse," Jane commanded.

Nothing. Mr. Hootenanny's feathers shimmered in the breeze.

"Stronger, like this. Mr. Hootenanny – mouse," Finch said. Mr. Hootenanny soared into the bush, emerged with a mouse and gulped it back.

"Maybe it's time to set him free." The owl flew back and perched on Aviary's arm. Finch and Mr. Hootenanny touched foreheads. Soft feathers against aged skin. I thought I saw tears gleam in Finch's eyes.

Todd leaped from behind a bush and interrupted what could have been an awkward moment. "Twins, nice to see you. I've spent the morning trailing Finch, keeping ear-one out for clues." Then he noticed Finch. "Sir, at your service ..." Todd recovered from his *faux pas*.

Finch didn't seem to notice. "Next time he'll listen to you, Jane. I'll get Hootenanny tethered and gather up Monsieur Vole for lunch."

"Nice one, Todd, you could have blown our undercover work," I said.

"I was just working with the owl; don't sweat it, Sis," said Jane.

"Stop defending him," I said. We were almost at the cottage.

"Like I say," Todd thumbed his ear as we approached the Finchs' cottage. "Seems he likes pencils."

"Pencils? Again with the pencils, Todd? Let me clue you in to something, pencil head. We need to find some answers and find them soon. There's a full-scale assault on the bird population just waiting to be launched by Finch and Vole. We need to find out why and how. You might want to use your smarminess to help the animal kingdom rather than yourself." My voice trembled. Wow, I thought *Jane* was the rebel twin with a lot of causes. The sound of construction was a low drone in the background.

"What Cyd means, Todd, is that we need to work together." Diplomatic twin to the rescue.

"That's not what I mean, Jane. I'm trying to rescue your cat, save the bird kingdom and this town from an imaginary advancing of insects that, according to you, will eat every shrub, leaf and blade of grass all because Yin caught a bird. Well, that's what they do Jane; they catch birds. Unless the world shifts on its axis and starts rotating backwards, cats will continue to catch birds."

Jane went pale at the mention of Yin. It was bad enough Yin was missing. I didn't have to rub it in like a grape juice stain on carpet.

"Girls, girls, let's not fight shall we?"

I slumped down on a stump. Jane sat beside me. She took out the water bottle and slid it to me. "It's been three days. Where is she?"

I took a deep swig and tossed it back to her.

"Todd is turning us against each other. Our mission here today is to infiltrate their home, find your cat, solve this crime, and then maybe we can go to the pool or something for a change," I said.

"Hello, did I hear something other than chirping out here?"

"Mrs. Finch, *enchanté*," Todd bowed, his classic greeting.

"Todd, Cyd and Jane, good to see you again. The beaks are simmering, come in."

She turned and disappeared into the thatched roof cottage.

"Beaks? Did she say *beaks*?" Jane asked.

"Sounded like beaks to me." Todd and Jane's grim faces matched mine. "Maybe it's her accent." I zipped up the backpack and swung it over my shoulder. "What's going on in there?"

We found Mrs. Finch in the kitchen. She was frying something in a pan. Her elbows were pulled up like wings, and her blouse billowed out at the arms.

"That smells lovely! What is it?" Jane sidled up beside her.

"What's that, dear? Can't hear you over the frying beaks."

"*Beaks?* That's what you're making?"

"That's right lassie, chicken potpie and beak soup."

Jane swung around with a horrified look on her face.

Aviary Finch and Souris Vole stormed into the cottage.

"You'll never get the plans through," Finch said.

"Once the birds are gone it will be ..." he spotted us. "Those children ..."

"Volunteers," Finch whispered into his ear.

"Volunteers, yes. Where would we be without you? I myself am a volunteer. Why, I donated the birdseed and volunteered my helicopters to distribute it all over the city for the birds."

"These wee bairns be hungry. Shall we sit down to eat?" Cygnet emerged from the kitchen with a huge pie.

"Of course, my sparrow." Aviary gave Cygnet a peck on the cheek. "All my Scottish favorites."

Six chairs surrounded the wooden table and we took a seat. I was elbow-to-elbow with Souris. Cygnet placed the pie in the middle of the table. A plate of what looked like black hockey pucks was beside it.

"What's that?" Jane asked.

"It's blood pudding, dear," Cygnet answered.

"Freaked-out twin, say what?'" I whispered to Todd.

"It doesn't *look* like dessert," said Jane.

"Blood pudding or black pudding isn't dessert." Finch reached across for the largest hockey puck. "It's also called blood sausage and it's a delicacy. It's made from onions, pig fat, oatmeal and pig's blood."

These are a few of my favorite things – not. I pushed my chair back from the table as the smells combined in my nose and churned in my gut.

"Yes, for my people as well. My grandmother made her version of blood sausage," added Souris as he handed me the plate.

"Pig's blood," I stammered, and blurted at the same time. "I had pig's blood for breakfast, I'm full up."

"Oh, lucky you, but you must try Cygnet's. It would make the Loch Ness Monster emerge from the water and walk to our cottage all the way from Scotland," said Aviary.

"Or maybe drown himself," I whispered to Jane.

"I'm a vegetable-tarian, er, vegetarian," said Jane.

Yeah, except for all that chicken, fish, and beef she eats. How convenient. I shot Jane the evil eye.

Souris held the plate beside me and waited for me to take some blood pudding. I was eyeball-to-hockey puck and needed to think detectively. Nancy Drew wouldn't be thrown by a little pig's blood and oatmeal. I straightened my back, gulped in a big mouthful of air, slid the smallest black hockey puck onto my fork, and put it on my plate.

"I'll split that with you," said Todd.

Finally, he was proving useful. I cut the puck in half, lifted the bigger half between my fork and knife, and forklifted it on to his plate.

I stared at my portion for a long time.

"You must have some beak soup then, Jane." Cygnet served up a bowl for her and set it at her place.

We peered at it and waited for beaks to pop out. The construction noise in the background stopped.

"Leek soup with rice. Just vegetables, nice fresh leeks grow outside the cottage. Go ahead, lassie."

We'd heard Cygnet clearly that time. "Leek soup?" Jane's face lit up. She plucked up her soupspoon and dug in. "Enjoy your blood pudding."

Aviary, Cygnet, and Souris tucked into the blood pudding like it was their birthday cake. I couldn't stall any longer. I broke off a corner with my fork and placed it on my tongue. The first taste sensation was blood. Like when you get a cut and lick the blood, but it was worse than that. It tasted like burnt blood. I bit down. It was crunchy. Crunchy oatmeal fried in burnt pigs blood. That just about summed it up. While I was grossed out, the writer in me thought of how to describe this on the blog.

Jane had overcome her fear of the beaks and inhaled the whole bowl of soup. She'd gotten past her vegetarianism as she maneuvered a big slab of meat pie onto her plate.

Cygnet remarked, "I'm glad you're enjoying your blood pudding, Cyd. Dig into the potpie. Nice young birds in there."

"Birds, did you say birds? Nice young birds?" said Jane, she halted in mid-chew.

We all looked at each other. I couldn't pull out the notebook to make notes so I would have to memorize this. It could be evidence.

"Yes, nice young birds. Very fresh, at the supermarket today. They got a fresh shipment in," replied Cygnet.

I slipped into detective mode. "But you said it was chicken."

"Chicken is a bird, my wee lassie." She talked to me like I speak to Yin when I explain why I don't want her to cough up any more hairballs into my shoes. "Chicken potpie."

Jane, Todd, and I looked at each other. Foiled by a thin Scottish bird-like woman and her chicken potpie.

Vole was close to licking his plate clean when Todd started interrogating him, er, engaging him in lively dinner conversation, as my mother would call it.

"Monsieur Vole ..." Todd commenced.

"Please, call me Souris," and he wiped his mouth with his napkin like a cat cleans its face.

"How long do you plan to stay in our quaint city?"

I kicked Todd under the table. Get to the point; I'd have had this guy stitched up by now and in the strait-jacket he deserved.

"I'll burrow back home as soon as my next project launches. Maybe a few months."

"What is that project?" Todd continued.

"Picture if you will," he spread his arms, "tropical trees for as far as the eye can see … a rainforest in the middle of the city … "

Jane and Todd were hanging on his every word like they were on the canopy of the rainforest.

To me, the guy sounded like an infomercial. I shot a sideways glance at Jane. "How do you plan to water it and keep it humid enough?" I asked. "The climate here is dry – that's going to waste a lot of water," I added.

"Well, we'll import the rainforest here …"

"But do you like birds? That's what I want to know."

Souris put the brakes on his sales pitch and shot me a sinister grin. It was as if he'd noticed me for the first time.

"Of course, I love birds." His beady eyes bored a hole through my forehead. "That's why I donated all that birdseed."

"And had it flown to the outskirts of the city." I gave him my best girl-detective glare. Jane and Todd cringed. All sounds of utensils clanging on plates stopped. All eyes were on me.

Cygnet plopped a bowl of granola in front of Souris, and he absentmindedly shoveled it into his mouth while he glared at me.

"I want all the birds of the city to enjoy the seed, not just the ones here."

He dug in with his paw, er, I mean hand, and held up a palm full of granola. He slammed his palm against his open mouth. The granola that didn't make the trip splattered across the table. His grin stretched out. Bits of granola flew out of his mouth while he chewed.

"Why not use it to feed the birds here, in the bird sanctuary? After all, that's what a sanctuary is for, to attract and protect the birds."

"It would be so lovely if the birds flew away." Aviary looked at the ceiling of the cottage as if it were imaginary clouds.

"Clamp your beak, Aviary. Enough with volunteer appreciation." Souris brushed the granola off his shirt and shuffled himself out of the chair. He leaned in close to me.

"The next time I see you … will be too soon," he sneered into my ear. "Keep your beak out of this. I wouldn't want your father to get in the way."

Jane's fork clanged on her plate. Todd's chair screeched across the floor as he pushed back from the table. I shivered even though it was hot and muggy in the cottage. Souris bolted for the door.

Chapter Eighteen
Tragedy or Comedy?

We convinced Dad it was take-your-twin-daugh-ters-and-their-annoying-teenage-sidekick-to-work day.

"Clues, you like that right? Clues. You girls are all about the clues, as they say, since you're detectives and all." I could see Dad's halfway mocking grin in the rear view mirror. He had no idea.

Dad was too friendly by half. It would be perfect spying time on Souris and Vole, though. Todd was driving E2 – the two evils. Jane and I brought our skateboards so we could dash after a couple of hours of observing E2.

"Girls, clamp your eyes on this Petri dish," said Dad.

Jane and I flanked him, one on each side. We peered into the small, round glass dish that scientists use in the lab to grow things, like cells and cultures.

"It's a regular apricot pit – the kind that grows around here, and I spliced in an apricot pit that Souris brought over from Europe. It will yield a super juicy apricot with a smaller pit."

"If the pit is smaller, will the cyanide be more concentrated?" Jane asked.

"Jane, I'm impressed: you've done your research. Yes, I suppose it would be more concentrated."

Not to be outdone, I piped up, "Why would they want a pit more concentrated with cyanide, Dad?"

"Souris and Vole are concentrating – get it, *concentrating*? – their efforts on the fruit. The pits will be ground up and used as compost. Recycling eh? You girls like that?"

"Or ground up and used as bird food," she whispered to me. I turned to see Jane scribbling in her notebook: *stronger cyanide equals more dead birds.*

"Right this way, sirs." Todd ushered in Vole and Souris with one of his bows.

"Yes, yes, ye wee lad, enough. Just let us through." Finch brushed past.

"Professor, so good to see you again." Souris held out a hand for Dad to shake. Then he presented Dad with a cookie tin. "Fresh apricot granola, I made it myself – for you, your lovely wife and girls."

Dad thanked him and handed me the tin. I pried it open and took a whiff. It smelled like apricot jam and oatmeal and that wasn't evil at all.

Then I noticed that Souris had a gym bag slung over his shoulder. I guessed it had more than smelly sweat socks in it, because it weighed him down on the one side.

We cornered Todd while the adult-greeting ritual took place. "We've cracked this mystery open like an apricot pit."

"That's great, twins, just great. Where did you say your mom is?"

"We didn't. If you're not going to take this seriously … " I said.

"Oh, I'm as serious as a paper cut on exam day. But you don't need me here supervising you."

"Supervising?" I glared.

"Cyd, let it go. Todd, down the hall, two doors to your left. Be back by lunch to drive those two home," Jane instructed.

Todd hightailed it out the door.

"What did you do that for?" I asked.

"We need some time to focus on the mystery. He's dragging us nowhere like Lucky when she gets a whiff of a squirrel."

Dad, Souris, and Finch stared at the Petri dish and talked in low tones. I sidled up to catch a listen. Jane held her pen at the ready, with an open notebook.

"But that could take years," Finch said.

"Only a couple of years." Dad glowed with pride.

"We don't have that kind of time; forget about the hybrid idea." Souris slung his gym bag on the table and it landed with a thud. "Is there a place we could grind these?" Out poured hundreds of apricot pits. They splayed across the table and some bounced off the floor.

"What?" Apricot pits cascaded onto Dad's shoes. "Grind?"

"For fertilizer, of course," Souris flipped our dad a rodent grin, " ... for the fruit trees."

Dad was flustered and pulled his feet up from under the pits. "Where did you get so many pits?"

"Some from my dear mother in France. She mailed them over," Vole said.

It would be a lot of postage for that package, I thought.

Vole added, "And some from fresh apricots here. My cook has been feeding me apricots for breakfast, lunch and dinner."

"There's a grinder on the third floor we could use."

Too friendly by three-quarters. Souris and Finch gathered up the pits, stuffed them back in the bag, and dashed out the door with Dad in tow.

"He's just like Lucky. Dad would follow anyone anywhere," I said.

Todd sauntered back in. "Lovely woman, your mother, and so smart."

"Let's go Todd. They've got Dad involved." I grabbed Todd by his collar and dragged him to the door.

We avalanched down the stairwell and met Dad, Souris and Finch coming off the elevator at the same time. They were trapped in their own vortex of bird nerdy-ness so we trailed behind them, close enough to hear, but not so close that they would notice us.

The machine was like a giant meat grinder. Souris poured handfuls of pits in the top, Dad pressed a button, and the sawdust powder of the ground pits fell into a bag Finch held at the other end. They went through these motions over and over. Lather, rinse, repeat. Scientist, land developer, and bird sanctuary owner. The Three Stooges of the adult world.

We were in the room at a safe distance from the machine. Jane's pen was at the ready. Todd seemed to be actually observing. And I was listening. The Three Stooges of the young detective world.

"Nice and fine, would mix in nicely with the birdseed," Souris said.

"You can't feed this to birds," Dad said over the buzz of the grinder. "It's like chocolate for dogs." He pressed the button.

Souris shoveled another handful of pits into the grinder. "Who said anything about dogs? It's the birds we need to take care of."

"Poison. This would poison birds, just like chocolate is poison for dogs," Dad shouted.

The machine ground to a halt as the last pit was pulverized.

"What will you use it for?" I piped up and stepped toward Dad.

Finch looked at me like he'd just noticed I was there. He addressed Dad and ignored me.

"Fertilizer for the trees. The apricots would be food; the ground pits, fertilizer," Finch added as he sealed off another bag and positioned an empty one under the spout.

"Right, fertilizer for the trees. You understand you can't feed this to birds," Dad confirmed. Doubt crept into his voice and tugged his smile down.

Souris nudged me out of the way, threw me a threatening glare and grabbed another handful of apricot pits. He'd seen the look on Dad's face.

"Professor, our aims are admirable. Keep those birdies happy. Right, Finch?" Souris shot Finch a look that said he'd better agree with him.

"Tweet, tweet," Finch said to my dad and Souris as he held up his arms.

Dad half-fake-grinned, and returned to the machine.

Finch turned to Souris. "... if you can stop them from making that noise, that 'tweet tweet,' I'll promise you all the haggis in Scotland." Dad didn't hear that part as he cleaned out the grinder.

Jane took notes of the whole conversation. She scooped up some of the apricot pit sawdust and squeezed it in her hand. She brushed it off her palm and went back to her notes.

We faded into the background as all three gathered up the sawdust and left. Dad motioned that he'd see us back at the house later.

Todd finally got a clue. "Those two are whacked out. They are trying to get rid of the birds."

"What took you so long to figure that out, Todd? That's why we're here," Jane shot back at him.

"I thought Finch was a little stressed out, doing some harmless bird-catching with a butterfly net. But these two are as serious as a power failure during a space-movie marathon. They want to rid the whole bird sanctuary of birds. But why?"

Jane examined her hand; it was red and raw where she had held the ground apricot pits.

The door swung open and banged against the wall. Finch stood with one arm stretched out and the other on his hip like he was onstage.

" 'A falcon, tow'ring in her pride of place, was by a mousing owl hawked at and killed.' Act II, scene iv, *Macbeth*." Finch took a bow, backed out of the room, and the door swung shut as if closed by some invisible breeze.

"Oh, that's just tragic," I said.

"Enough with the Shakespeare already," Jane slammed shut her notebook.

Chapter Nineteen
More Cats Equals Fewer Birds

Jane and Todd scoured the 'net for some connection to the clues we had, as I flipped through my Dad's dog-eared copy of Shakespeare's *Macbeth*. Three glasses of cherry lemonade perched on the patio table. I'd been reading *Macbeth* since we saw the play in England last year. We were on the back deck and Jane had the laptop. Todd was finally on board with solving this mystery, now that he saw Finch and Vole intended to kill birds and deceive a well-meaning scientist in the process.

I scanned the introduction. "There's a rumor that the play *Macbeth* has a curse on it. Every time the play was staged, things would go wrong in the theatre." I tossed the book on the patio table. "Is anybody listening to me?" Lucky jumped up and put her head on my lap. Lucky, a girl detective's best friend.

"Yeah, yeah," Todd waved his arm like he was flagging a taxi, but his eyes were still clamped on the screen. "We get it. Plays, ghosts, curses."

"Wait until you see what we found, Cyd," added Jane.

So, they were friends all of a sudden? Where did that leave me? I scratched between Lucky's ears.

"We're on Vole's company homepage. He's talking about a big development in our town, but he can't say anything about it until the permits go through city council," Todd said.

"Well, there are no by-laws against planting trees – even tropical ones – so it can't be the tropical rainforest project," I interjected.

"Maybe it has something to do with the land the bird sanctuary is on," Jane added.

"But they can't build on a protected area," Todd said.

"Oh, you're right, Todd," Jane gushed.

"Okay, what just happened here? You two were fighting like hawks a while ago. Now you're all lovey-dovey."

They turned and smiled at me. "We're trying to solve the mystery is all," Jane said. "Teamwork, Cyd; get on board. You know what they say, 'There's no I in team.' The sooner we solve this mystery the sooner we get Yin back – I know they've got her." Jane's voice wavered from cheery to sad.

"Jane, we already figured out they can't build on a protected area. Let's go back to the Shakespeare clue. We're writers after all."

"Right," my sister called over her shoulder at me, then turned back to the computer. "Todd, after this we need to update our blog."

"*Our* blog, Jane. Yours and mine. Not yours and Todd's."

"Cyd, didn't you hear me? We're a team in this mystery now."

It seemed there was also no "Cyd" in team. Breathe, I told myself. "The important thing is to get Yin back and to save the bird kingdom. Or is that the bird song-dom? Beak-dom?" I asked.

Jane giggled. I exhaled a bit.

"That's me done surfing," said Todd. He swung his chair around away from the computer and the patio table.

"You sound like Finch," I shot back.

"That reminds me," Jane said, still at the computer. "I just wanted to check the animal shelter site again. Maybe there's a way to get Contessa back, like, maybe on being-nice-to-old-people grounds or something." She clicked on the shelter site she had bookmarked. "Holy catnip, look at this."

Todd and I peered over her shoulder. Cat pictures covered the screen. Every picture had an *adopted* banner across it.

"What's up with that?" I asked. "They can't all be adopted."

Jane clicked on a photo to expand it. "Adopted by Aviary and Cygnet Finch." She read. She clicked on the next one. "Adopted by Aviary and Cygnet Finch." She clicked on the next and the next. "What's going on? They were all adopted by Aviary and Cygnet Finch."

Jane turned to face us. We both looked at Todd.

"Do you know anything about this?" I grilled him.

He shrugged and backed away. "No, they don't tell me anything."

"Oh, but I thought you ran the place, Todd." I took a step toward him. "Isn't that what you told us? You have the key to the office, Todd." I took another step and was right in front of him. "Looks like Finch is back on the 'cat-killing bird idea.' "

"Back off, Cyd," Jane piped up.

"Look, I didn't suspect Finch was serious about the 'more cats equals fewer birds' strategy." Todd ducked behind Jane as he defended himself. He knocked over all three glasses of cherry lemonade. The juice spilled like blood on the plastic patio table. Jane snatched up the laptop.

The three of us paused, mesmerized as it dripped over the side. Lucky, stood under the table and caught the drips like rainwater.

Todd plowed ahead with his defense. "I'm clued into the new plan – full-steam ahead on the apricot-pit sawdust."

"Looks like Finch is serious – dead-birdly serious. He's not taking any chances that there will be a single bird left in that sanctuary." I slumped down in the patio chair and Lucky bounded up into my lap.

"It's okay, Cyd." Jane got a sponge from the kitchen and sopped up the juice. She sat down in the chair next to me. Todd backed away in case I went off again. "We'll crack this case faster than Finch and Vole can eat through an apricot to get the pit," Jane said.

Okay, Jane wasn't great with the one-liners, but it calmed me down long enough to realize why I was so mad. "I want Yin back. And even though I'm not crazy about animals like you are, I'm not going to stand around and wait for them to be killed."

"Technically," said Todd, "you're sitting."

I raised one eyebrow in a threatening sneer. "Technically, the option of going all Lady Macbeth on you two, or just Todd, is looking better."

"I've cleaned up the juice but the cherry-red stain is still there," Jane said. "Mom's going to kill us if she sees that."

"Here let me have a go at it." I grabbed the sponge and scrubbed. "Out, danged spot! Out, I say!"

Todd and Jane stared at me like I was as crazy as a finch, a Shakespeare-spouting Aviary Finch.

Lucky broke the tension when she dropped a half-eaten tennis ball, covered in juice, at my feet.

"We have to crack this mystery. Why did Finch adopt all those cats? We just need to think on it a bit." Jane grabbed her notebook off the computer table. She read from it like Mom from her to-do list.

"So here's how we'll roll. Todd's going to hang out with Vole at his office – you know, job-shadow him – and dig around for info."

"That job-shadow thing is great for gaining access to solve mysteries." He smiled at Jane, who continued:

"Then we meet up tonight at the bird sanctuary, break into Finch's office, and rifle through his files." She glanced over at me. "And we'll find out what's up with all the cats."

Todd pulled on the keys until the wire that held them was stretched to the end, and then let go of them. He groaned when the wire snapped against his leg.

***

It was easier to sneak out of the house with our volunteer job. I felt a little guilty when we lied to Mom and Dad, but they weren't a fan of our mysteries and the fates of the bird and cat worlds were at stake. Well, maybe that's an exaggeration, but we still wanted to solve the mystery and get Yin back. Parents are pretty clueless when kids are trying to save various animal worlds.

We told our parents that we were going to study owl activity at night. That we were doing a bird count of owls to see how many of them were in this eco-system. They lapped that one up like Yin when I squeezed out the water from the tuna can into her cat food bowl.

Dad dropped us off.

It was creepy dark at night. There were no lights on the grounds of the sanctuary, because it was, well, a sanctuary. The eerie haze of the lights from downtown glowed in the distance.

"Vole showed me the plans for the condominium development at his office today, and he was really sneaky about where it would be located in the city. I think we need to get a better look at the blueprints we saw last time we rifled through his desk." Todd held up the key like a four-year-old shows off a soccer trophy.

"Enough with the dramatics, Shakespeare – just open the door, already. This chirping is freaking me out." The sounds of birds chirping echoed against the sounds of the trees creaking. Anyone who said nature was relaxing never volunteered at a bird sanctuary at night.

Todd switched off the alarm system and fumbled with the key. We entered the visitor's center. He flicked the light on and it hummed before illuminating the center. I shielded my eyes from the shock of the brightness after the pitch of the blackness. The air became dustier as we made our way to Finch's office. The three of us stood at the door and surveyed the room. It was much the same way as we had left it. Jane glanced under the desk as if she'd find Yin the same way we found Contessa Cuddles.

"Let's get to it …" I strode to the desk and unrolled the first blueprint. It was the same one with the trees. I flung that to the ground as Jane unrolled the next blueprint and laid it flat on the desk.

"It's an office building." Todd and I peered over her shoulder. She leaned in to examine the blueprints. "No, it looks like a high-rise apartment, see this nice courtyard with the trees, and shops on the main floor. Maybe a condominium complex."

"Why would the director of the bird sanctuary have these plans on his desk?" I asked.

"Maybe it's a development the bird sanctuary has been asked to comment on, you know, like for the environmental assessment. Even if the development was on the other side of the city and the migratory birds would pass over it, the city would have to consult with the sanctuary to make sure there would be no impact on the birds," said Jane, the Queen of the By-Law.

"You can't tell where it is, really. It could be any-where in the city, right?" asked Todd.

Jane wasn't buying that; she had her sleuth on. She combed every square inch of that blueprint while I held it open.

The light was dimmer in Finch's office. Jane snapped on the desk lamp, pulled out her key chain, and clicked the end of her penlight. She was on fire, girl-detective-wise.

"Here it is, Cyd." She shone the light on the bottom of the page. I bent to scope out the tiniest of letters. The lettering was miniature, but the words were unmistakable.

" 'Wildwood Bird Sanctuary Project,' " I read.

"Gimme that." Todd grabbed it and held it under the desk lamp. He struggled to keep both sides of the blueprint flat while zoning in on the petite print. "This can't be right."

Jane held one end and they rolled it out again. "It says 'Wildwood Bird Sanctuary,' and it's a condo com-plex – on the Wildwood Bird Sanctuary."

I leaned in to examine the blueprints. There was no mistaking it.

Jane let the blueprint snap back into a roll. We faced each other in a detective huddle; it was like football, but without the sports part.

"That brochure Kitty showed me ... " I rummaged in the backpack. "Where did I put that."

"But we know they can't build here. What are they playing at?" Jane asked.

"They swore it would be somewhere else," Todd mumbled half to himself and half out loud.

"What do you mean?" I started to say.

The visitor center door slammed shut. We froze.

Vole's voice echoed from the visitor center. "Well, you must have left the lights on, because it's lit up brighter than the Hindu festival of Diwali."

"I was sure I turned them off. That's not me wasting funding. Ye must have left them on."

Their arguing over the use of renewable resources was our ticket to hide. Jane and I dived under the giant desk and Todd headed for a plant in the corner. The blueprints were knocked to the ground in the dash to hide.

"Todd, what are you doing here?" Vole's voice accused him. "At this hour of the night."

I spied Todd from my hiding place and Vole came into view.

"Sir et Monsieur, just putting in a few extra hours. Thought I'd do a count of the owls, hoot, hoot." Todd wrung his hands together, then, wiped the sweat off his brow.

"Good idea, my lad. The fewer hoots the better," said Finch.

"Other than from the splendid Mr. Hootenanny, of course," Todd said.

Flattery will get Todd everywhere, I thought.

"Yes, brilliant display of initiative, my boy," Vole said.

Todd relaxed.

Vole put his hand on Todd's shoulder, and leaned in close to his ear. "But then why would you be in here? I don't see any owls, do you?" Vole squeezed Todd's shoulder with his fingers. "Why not outside with your feathered friends?"

Todd crumbled under the pressure. "Well, uh … " He wrenched his shoulder out of the rodent hold.

He moved toward the desk and blocked my view of E2. I heard the rustling of paper.

"I just thought I'd clean up the office. Get these blueprints out of view." Todd grabbed the one off the floor, rolled it up, stepped over to Vole, and presented the blueprint to him. Vole came back into my view.

Vole winked.

Jane and I exchanged a glance in the small space under the desk. What was up with that? I inched my fingers out and grabbed the other blueprint.

"I can take these off you," Vole said. "The place looks much cleaner already. Good job, Todd. Wouldn't want these to get into the wrong hands."

"Yes, the professors' girls fancy themselves as detectives." Todd laughed. "I'll keep their snoopy noses busy in the animal hospital cleaning cages."

"You're going places, my boy." Vole patted Todd on the shoulder. Todd beamed back and all three of them left the room. "We need to step things up a few notches," I heard them say as the door to the bird sanctuary closed.

Jane and I emerged from under the desk.
"He gave them the plans," said Jane.
"Chill out, sis," I pulled a rolled up, folded over, and generally squished blueprint from under my shirt. "Vole's got the one with the trees. We've got the one with the building."
"We can take it to City Hall," Jane grinned.
"Yeah, that worked so well last time we involved the authorities." Jane was right, though; this kind of evidence could stop the development in its tracks of mud. I shoved the blueprint into Jane's backpack as I heard Todd's footsteps coming back.

Chapter Twenty
Hostile Bird Nerd, Handle with Care

"Okay, that's them taken care of." Todd brushed his hands as if they were covered in dirt.

"What's up with you?" Jane pounced on him. "Why'd you give him the plans?"

"A, I was caught. B, they were his company's plans anyway, and I'm sure they have other copies; and C, now we can search without them coming back."

"Well, that seems half-likely." I glanced at Jane, and she nodded.

"Well, they'll be shocked when they find out they don't have the real plans. Cyd's got the building plans and they have the tropical orchard plans," Jane said.

"What do you mean?" Todd's jaw clenched and the expression drained from his face.

"Why did you tell him that?" I threw the question at Jane.

"We're a team, Cyd. He's part of the team now, remember?"

"He just gave them what he thought were the real plans. We still don't know if we can trust him."

"I said, *What do you mean*?" Todd punctuated every word louder.

We stopped our twin twitter and swung around to face him. He looked scared and angry. It gave me a bad case of the creeps. But I wasn't going to back down now.

I stepped closer to him and shoved my snout in his face. "The old switcheroo, Todd. The plans are well-hidden." I grabbed Jane's backpack and slung it on my back.

"Give them to me, now." He grabbed for the backpack. "They don't belong to me. Finch and Vole will be smoking-mad if those plans get lost. They'll know it was me."

I jumped back and out of his way. Jane cowered behind me.

"Like you say, they probably have lots of copies," I said.

"They trusted me. I want that copy back. All copies outside of the office need to be destroyed." Todd was the most shocked by what leaked out of his mouth. Jane and I stood stunned. He rushed toward me.

"Back off, bird nerd." Dead silence in the room.

It was pitch-black outside. Todd stared at me. The only sounds were the night chirping of the birds. No one else was around. No one to rescue us. I scanned Finch's desk and grabbed a stapler. It looked like it was out of the Stone Age but it could bean the daylights out of Todd. The standoff continued.

Jane chirped up from behind me, "Todd, whose side are you on? Did they ask you to destroy this copy? Is that why we're here?"

"Uhh ... I'm just messing with you twins." Todd relaxed his stance but his voice cracked as he said it. "Like the salami thing." He stepped toward me.

I waved the stapler at him like a sword. "It doesn't seem like you're messing with us. It sounds like you're serious."

"I just don't want things to get out of hand. If Vole notices the plans are gone, things could get ugly." Todd rubbed his shoulder. "He needs those plans."

A loud meow sound echoed from Jane's pocket. She'd recorded Yin's meow as her ring tone. Jane flipped it open. "Hi, yup ... yup, north door, five minutes. We'll be there." She flipped it shut with a snap of the wrist. "Dad was in the 'hood. It's dark out, so he decided to pick us up," she shorthanded for me.

"We're going to have to take this up at another time," I said, as Jane and I inched toward the door together with the backpack squeezed between us.

Todd blocked the doorway with his body. It was a stare-down.

"Give him the plans, Cyd. We don't want him to get in trouble."

I looked at Todd, and then my simpering sis. I slowly shifted the backpack from my back and hugged it to my chest in a death grip. I locked eyes with him.

Todd half-heartedly moved out of the way. He bowed and swooshed his arm as if to show us the way to leave. There wasn't a smile on his face for miles.

We broke into a run when we hit the exit.

"What crawled into his gullet and died?" I asked.

"He can still be in the mystery, right, Cyd?" I heard Jane yell as we ran in the breeze.

***

The image of Todd the hostile bird nerd kept me awake. What was his angle? Wondering about this, I snagged a few hours' sleep at most.

In the morning I hopped out of bed and dove into cyberspace to get at those city by-laws.

Jane was furiously texting someone.

I searched the city's site and found the by-laws. " 'Wildwood Bird Sanctuary.' Here it is, Jane." I clicked on the link. " 'Created in 1930 as a special order of council to save the area from development.' You were right, it's a protected area," I called over my shoulder.

"Just got a text from Todd," Jane said.

"I'll print out the exact order in council to look at the wording." I clicked on the link and it went to an unpopulated webpage. *Orders in Council for this year are in the archives and are not available online,* I read.

"He's really sorry about what happened last night."

"Not available online? Oh, that's just so 1996."

"Turns out he had sunstroke."

"What?" we said simultaneously.

"Archives: that's so primitive, everything on paper. Why can't we download it to our blog?" Jane asked.

"Sunstroke! It was darker than a bat's wing last night – there *was* no sun," I said.

"He wants back in the mystery," Jane said.

"No way. There wasn't even moonlight." I grabbed the digital camera. "He couldn't even get moonstroke if there was such a thing."

"He wants to get his sleuth back on."

I swung to face Jane. "Whose side are you on?"

Jane half-giggled, saw I was serious, and said, "Come on, Cyd. He was just nervous, that's all. He's under a lot of pressure."

"Pressure? From what, being a teenage bird nerd? Forget it. What if he knows where your cat is and isn't saying? Hand me your notebook. We're headed for the archives."

Jane handed me the notebook.

I shoved it in the backpack, next to the copy of *Macbeth*, zipped it up, slung it on my shoulder, and faced Jane. She stood there with a look on her face like I had just killed her pet frog.

She protested, "Of course I'm on your side. We're twins. But Cyd, everyone deserves a second chance. Even the bird nerd."

"Why do you always do this to me?"

"We're more likely to find Yin if all three of us are involved." Jane pulled her best two-minutes-younger-twin pout.

"All right, but only one second chance. Tell him to meet us at the archives." I sighed.

Jane squeezed me. Then dashed off a text on her phone. She scratched at her palm like Lucky digging up a bone.

***

"Todd looks like the Blackburnian Warbler, a.k.a. the orange-throated warbler, in that orange-and-yellow shirt." I needed to get off this bird mystery soon. I knew way too much about birds.

"I know. He looks great, right?"

"What's up, twins? Ready to crack this mystery open like a bird beak against a high-rise window?" Todd was his regular self again, and by that, I mean annoying. "Look, Cyd, I wanted to apologize …"

"Forget it, Todd. We just need to know if you're here for the birds or the culprits."

"I won't even mention the blueprints again – promise. Here, let me carry some of your stuff." Todd took Jane's backpack from her. Jane grinned like a ninny.

The archive building was as grey as a mid-winter's day. There were no windows, and inside it was filled with rows and rows of filing cabinets. But first we had to get past the archivist. He was twice as old and four times as dusty as any of the documents there. He looked like a professor who'd time-traveled from the last century.

"No kids allowed. Get lost."

"But we're here to locate a by-law," Jane squeaked.

"Go to the school library and look up by-laws there. I don't want clumsy kid fingers all over my archives."

I took what I hoped was an official tone. "School's closed. We're here on official business. We're investigating a land use bylaw and need to see the original order in council."

"The lives of birds are at stake," piped up Jane.

Oh, here we go with the whole animal-loving thing.

"I wouldn't care if you were the mayor. No fingerprints on my papers."

"Maybe you should digitize the papers. Then they'd last forever, and anyone could look at them," Jane suggested.

"Maybe you should go play a computer game or search the world ... wide ... web." The archivist stretched the words out mockingly.

"My good man," Todd said in his fake Shakespeare voice. "I work for the Wildwood Bird Sanctuary." He flipped the archivist his identification card. "I'm here on official business. We need to see the original document that created the sanctuary."

"Well, why didn't you say so instead of letting these kids bug me?"

"Volunteers, our youth corps of volunteers. They have so much to learn, but under my tutelage ... "

"Quit your yapping and follow me. You're a real pain in my tailbone."

The archivist and I had one thing in common: we both found Todd infuriating.

Mr. Grumpy led us to a back room. There was one lightbulb and a ceiling fan that was busted. The room was darker and dustier than the rest of the building. There were four filing cabinets, all marked *Wildwood Bird Sanctuary*.

"Don't mess things up. You can take copies if you can get the photocopier to work." With that, the archivist left us in there.

"Tutelage, Todd?" I grilled him.

"Stop arguing and start searching. There are tons of documents to go through here," Jane said.

"We've got a few things to teach you about sleuthing."

We each took a filing cabinet.

Each file released a puff of dust that I hoped didn't contain an ancient curse like when they opened King Tut's tomb.

"I'm getting closer. Here are all the records of the consultation they did back in the olden days before declaring it a sanctuary," Jane said.

"And here are the earlier drafts of the order in councils," Todd added.

I'd make detectives out of these two yet.

"Here it is: *Final Order in Council creating the Wildwood Bird Sanctuary,*" Todd declared.

"Read it out loud."

He skimmed through. " 'This land will remain a bird sanctuary indefinitely.' "

"That means forever," I said.

" 'The land can only be used for other purposes, such as development, if the land can no longer sustain the bird population.' " Todd stopped reading. His face turned as ash-grey as the walls of the room.

"What does that mean?" asked Jane.

"It means fewer birds equals a big honking condominium complex," I said. "If the land isn't used for a bird sanctuary anymore, they can develop on it."

"They need to kill all the birds to get their plans through," Jane said.

"Now, let's not be hasty," said Todd. He tried to shove the paper back in the file.

"That's why they don't want anyone to see the plans. They need to get rid of all the birds first."

I pried it out of the packed file and tried not to rip it.

Jane and I locked eyes. "Let's do this."

Jane took a picture, with her cell phone, of each page of the order in council. She e-mailed it to our home computer.

We left Todd in the dusty chamber and bee-lined it out the door and onto our bikes.

Chapter Twenty-One
Double-Crossed by an Apricot Pit

"We need to get this archival document to the mayor," Jane declared.

As soon as we we got home, my sister printed out the photo of the order in council that she'd e-mailed from the archives. She scratched at her palm, which was now as red as a cinnamon heart candy.

I tucked the printout into her notebook and shoved it in my backpack. For once I agreed with her going-to-the-authorities idea, but we weren't ready to tell our parents. We'd texted Mom and told her we were going to look for Yin again.

We were halfway out the back door when a piece of lavender notepaper, left on the kitchen table, caught my eye. It was a note written by Dad. Unlike Mom, he believed in recycling and was using up old notepaper that our Grandma in England gave us. It smelled faintly of rose petals. The note was short and to the point, the exact opposite of Dad who was tall and tended to drone on at times.

The note read: *Dog walked and fed. Mom at faculty meeting. I'm at the university with Finch and Vole. Left-over ribs in fridge. Later, gators.*

I grabbed Jane by the T-shirt. "Change of plans. City Hall will have to wait. Dad's at the university with Finch and Vole."

That was all Jane needed. She vaulted up the stairs and headed toward our room. She flashed our security passes on her way back out the door.

Jane texted as she hopped on her bike. "Todd will meet us there," she reported. "Vole's going to be mad about the plans and the break-in last night, no telling what he'll do."

"We don't want Dad ground into their plans like apricot pit on shag carpet," I yelled into the wind as my bike shook and my stomach clenched. I pushed down on my bike pedals; with every push we were closer to finding Dad.

When we reached the university, we could hear them from down the hall: Finch's Scottish Accent; Souris's slightly European lilting voice; and our dad's professor murmur.

Todd waited at the elevator and fell into step behind us.

We crouched by the door, which was open a crack, and peeked in to see a burlap sack filled with ground-up apricot pits. All three of them were gathered around the table.

"So you see," Dad peered at an apricot pit he held in front of his face, "this pit ground up would be super-concentrated with cyanide. So you're going to have to be careful that this fertilizer isn't used anywhere the birds might eat, or where children play."

"Och, the birds will eat anything, and now they chirp all night, ever since the construction … "

"That's enough, Aviary," Souris cut him off. "The professor isn't interested in that."

No, Dad wasn't interested, but we were. Jane scribbled so quickly her pencil flew off the page and crashed to the ground.

Aviary opened the door with a flourish. "Todd and the wee lasses, what are ye doing here?"

"Just came to see the esteemed professor at work." Todd jumped up, tucked in his shirt and smoothed down his hair.

We ran to stand next to Dad.

"Girls, I left you a note. What's up?"

"They're not who they say they are, Dad. They've got Yin," Jane said.

Souris's mouth tightened into a sneer.

Dad shot an uncomfortable glance at me. "Girls, we talked about this. Mr. Finch and Monsieur Vole are not involved in the kidnapping."

"Dad, it's about more than the cats. It's about the birds as well," I said. "Ask Todd. He knows what we're talking about."

Todd was quieter than a dove.

"Todd, do you have what I asked for?" Vole drew out his words, but they had an edge to them.

Todd crossed the floor and stood beside Finch and Vole. He handed them the rolled up, folded and generally squished blue print. "They had the blueprint and know about the land use by-law." He presented the copy of the faded by-law.

"Todd!" Jane's voice filled with tears, and I don't think they were for Yin.

"Next time, twins, get a lock for that backpack."

"Ah, thank you, Todd," Vole smirked. "You were helpful removing the cats at the cat show, we couldn't have done it alone."

"Todd! Not Yin. How could you?" Jane cried.

I spat out, "I knew you were a double agent, Todd. You double-crossing double crosser."

"What's going on here?" Dad asked.

"I'll tell you what," I said. "If the apricot pits don't kill the birds, the cats Finch and Vole kidnapped will. Then they will be able to develop that land because it will no longer be a bird sanctuary."

"You can't use science for evil purposes." Dad seemed shocked that someone would even think about that. "I thought you were building a tropical paradise for birds?"

"That's just what they told City Hall. They plan to tear down the seniors' cottages. They're already advertising it – a high-rise condominium building on the edge of the sanctuary," I said. "That's where those construction noises are coming from."

"Not if I can help it." Dad pulled out his cell phone.

"Todd, go," Souris commanded.

Todd thrust his hand into the sack of ground up apricot pits. He bounded around the table and threw a handful of the apricot sawdust in Dad's eyes.

Dad screamed in anguish and rubbed his eyes. He stumbled, searching for the sink.

Todd rushed back behind Souris and Finch, rifled through a cupboard, and pulled out a rope. He and Souris advanced toward Dad. He couldn't defend himself because he was writhing in pain. I smacked Souris and Todd with my backpack. Jane retreated to the corner, crying. They grabbed Dad and tied him up.

" 'Fair is foul, and foul is fair,' as the witches said in Act I, scene i," said Finch to the ceiling tiles.

Souris and Todd yanked my arms and tied me up. I struggled, but they were stronger.

"You won't get away with this," I screamed, and bit Todd's shoulder. "People know where we are."

"You mean like your mother? Isn't she in a faculty meeting, and didn't you tell her we were going searching for that bag of fur you call a cat? You might want to put a password on your text messages as well." Todd grinned. It was the start of an evil grin – he had learned well.

All I had left were insults. "Todd, you are worse than a computer virus."

"Oh, Todd, why?" Jane whimpered between sobs. She rubbed at her inflamed hand, then stared at it. "Dad, it's poison for birds and for kids. Look at my hand! I held some of the ground apricot pits the other day and now look at it. There are lots of kids in the sanctuary."

Then they dragged Jane out of the corner and tied her up. I noticed that Todd didn't tie her as tightly as he did me.

"Todd, I thought you were my friend," she sniveled.

"I'll scream my head off," Dad threatened. His eyes were red and puffed out.

"Not with a mouthful of ground-up apricot pit to chew on, you won't." Souris came over with a big handful and shoved it into my dad's mouth.

Jane and I screamed out for help.

I caught Finch's eye. There was a glimmer of doubt. He mumbled, " 'Double, double toil and trouble; fire burn and cauldron bubble.' " Then he stood on his left leg and shook his head. He pounded on one ear like he was trying to drain water out after swimming.

Dazed and confused, he spoke again. "No more killing, no more murder." He stepped forward, thrust his arm in the air and quoted again: " '… this is more strange than such a murder is.' " He peered around, hopeful for applause.

All eyes were on him and all mouths were gaping. Except Dad's – he was trying to spit out the ground up apricot pits.

"*Macbeth* Act III, scene iv. That's it!" I exclaimed. "Finch isn't evil."

"Stop it, stop talking. Todd, fill her mouth with sawdust," Souris commanded.

"You put one finger in my mouth and I'll chomp down to the bone." I'd learned that one from Lucky.

Todd didn't move. All eyes were on me and I had to make this good.

"Listen. When Jane and Todd were updating the blog I deciphered the clues in Shakespeare. I read the play a couple of times and studied the plot analysis."

Dad grunted, nodded his head toward Souris and spat the apricot pit sawdust out. "Cyd, this is no time for Language Arts class."

I steamrolled on. I wouldn't have their attention much longer. "Earlier in Act II, scene iv, people talked about all the strange things that had happened since Macbeth murdered the King. Back in the day, they thought their king was connected to nature. If the king was good, nature would cooperate. If the king was bad then things would go wacky in nature. So the line Finch spewed last time we were in the lab: 'On Tuesday last, a falcon towering in her pride of place was by a mousing owl hawked at and killed.' It means that this is the opposite of what happens in nature. Which is exactly what murdering a king would be, the opposite because he's supposed to die naturally and not be murdered."

They listened but Todd ran his fingers through the apricot pit sawdust. He clutched a handful and then let it slip between his fingers. Then he checked for an allergic reaction.

Jane clued in and zipped her tears. A determined look replaced the sniveling one on her face. Jane slipped her ropes off and grabbed my backpack. The dog-eared copy of *Macbeth* was inside. She skimmed the introduction.

I rushed on. "So a noble bird – the falcon – is killed by an owl, which represents Macbeth, once a loyal servant of the king. So, that's the opposite of what is supposed to happen. Finch is the owner of the bird sanctuary and killing birds is the opposite of what should happen in nature *because Finch is all about the birds.*"

Jane took over. "I didn't sleep through *Macbeth* last summer. Finch is the loyal owl that is now killing the noble birds he is supposed to take care of – the opposite of what is supposed to happen. Finch knows it; he's not evil. He's *Macbeth.*"

"Once they're gone, you can use the land and I can have silence." Finch slumped down and cried.

"But Souris and Todd, now they're Evil Squared," I said, ending the twin soliloquy. A soliloquy is usually a speech by one person, except in the event of twin detectives using Shakespeare for good rather than tragic reasons.

Souris snapped, "I won't hear any more of this. Come, Todd. Tonight we release the claws."

Todd tied up the burlap sack, slung it over his shoulder and puppy-dogged behind Souris out the door. He glanced back once, locked eyes with Jane, and looked away.

Finch lay crumpled up. We were barely tied up and Dad was fed up.

He spat out the last of the apricot pit dust. "Ugh, that's worse than your mother's crumble. But don't tell her that."

Chapter Twenty-two
Falcon and Owl

Aviary Finch untied us between crying jags. Dad rinsed the last of the ground apricot pit from his mouth and phoned the police.

I said, "They are not going to help us, Dad. Don't you remember what happened in the last mystery? Nobody believed us."

"They'll believe an adult."

Finch cried himself empty. We dried his tears, dusted him off, and plopped him in a chair.

"What's the plan?" I asked.

"Birds," he flapped his hands. "Poison," and he clutched at his throat like he was dying. "Cats!" He clawed the air like, well, like a cat.

Dad pointed out, "He's no good to us like this. We need to get down there."

Dad alternately fumed and hummed along to the elevator music. He was on hold with the cops. I flapped my arms and mouthed *bird sanctuary*, and Jane and I bolted for the elevators before Dad could stop us.

The warm night air hit us as we hopped on our bikes and headed to the bird sanctuary. We had less than an hour before we'd be in total darkness.

We heard the symphony of cat and bird noises before we saw anything. We whizzed past the Finchs' cottage and screeched to a halt at the visitor center. Todd struggled to upright a floodlight on a steel beam. There were five more like it. He shoved a giant plug into an outlet on the outside of the visitor center and the sanctuary grounds lit up. Todd saw us. He thrust both hands into the bag of ground apricot pits and flung handfuls to the birds that were swooping down to eat it. Songbirds sleep at night – the lights would wake them up. The bird kingdom was in the wrong time zone.

"Stand back, twins, and nobody gets hurt."

"Stop trying to sound like you're on a TV detective show and tell us what's up."

"I'm in too deep. Save yourselves."

"Oh, Todd," Jane wailed.

Holy Shakespeare – I didn't know if this was a comedy or a tragedy, but I needed to lower the curtain on this production.

Beep … beep …beep. The familiar sound of a truck backing up. I swerved around to see a moving van backing toward me. A caterwauling seeped out from the back. I leaped out of the way just as the truck rolled over and parked where I'd been standing.

"Jane, the cats are in the truck," I yelled over the beeping sound.

The engine moaned to a stop and Souris bounded out of the driver's seat. He raced to the back of the truck and threw open the door. The cats bolted out. Some of them cowered from the light, but most of them dashed straight into the woods for cover. Yin's half-black forehead caught my eye.

"Jane, it's Yin! She's all right – I saw her."

Jane came over and stood by me. We watched the action.

Then the birds started up, squawking and chirping like their lives depended on it. Well, I guess it did. The birds flapped in slow motion, most likely feeling the effects of the poison. And the cats did what cats do. They stalked and pounced. Claws and feathers filled the air. High-pitched bird screeches mixed in the air with wailing cat meows. Blood spilled as cats dragged their prey deeper into the woods to eat it.

Then something strange happened. Nature fought back. The air cleared and silence prevailed. The sun sank lower and the air chilled.

Souris strode to the killing fields where the bird carcasses lay near the ground apricot pits. The cats scrammed. He circled like a rodent looking for his burrow and sniffed the air. He stood in the middle of the circle and raised his arms. "It's mine, all mine," he shouted to no one in particular.

Then a swooshing sound. Then again. We peered at the sky. A magnificent owl swooped down. It was Mr. Hootenanny. Predator became prey.

Jane whistled the way Aviary showed her. She pulled her jacket down over her hand and Mr. Hootenanny landed hard on her arm. She winced and struggled to hold her arm steady.

Sirens screamed into the night. The police, fire-fighters, and animal protection services – and Dad – all arrived at the same time. Finch cringed in the back seat of Dad's car.

Dad and Finch raced out of the car to see Jane and Mr. Hootenanny eyeball-to-eyeball. Vole stomped on the apricot sawdust and danced around.

"Stars, hide your fires! Let not light see Vole's black and deep desires," Finch moaned.

"Mr. Hootenanny – Souris," Jane commanded. The bird took flight, swooped down once, flew back up, gained speed and swooped down a second and final time.

Souris swiveled in his victory dance just in time to feel the full force of the bird knock him down. The owl pinned Souris to the ground with his claws. It took flight again, but Souris didn't move. The owl returned to Jane's arm.

"Mr. Hootenanny – Souris," Jane repeated.

The owl swooped up and dive-bombed Souris again. Mr. Hootenanny stood on Souris and glared at us. Souris didn't move and neither did the hoot.

"I thought the command word was 'mouse?' " I asked Jane.

"I taught the owl French." Jane grinned.

Fair is foul, and foul is fair, as the guy with the puffy pants wrote.

"Are you girls all right?" Dad yelled as he ran to us. He gathered us under his wings. "What happened …" he stopped talking when he saw Souris pinned down by the owl.

"It's over for him, Dad," I said.

At the sound of Dad's voice, Yin emerged from the trees and popped her head out of the bushes. Jane bolted and gathered her up. Yin purred and sunk deeper into Jane's arms.

"I've never been so happy to see this hairball in my life." I gave Yin a scratch between the ears.

Cygnet had heard the noise from the cottage and stood by Aviary's side. They stood, arm-in-arm, and surveyed the damage to the sanctuary. The wail of the sirens died down.

Animal protection services cleaned up the dead birds and searched for the cats. The owl returned to Finch's arm when Souris was heaved into the ambulance. Todd helped them clean up and then he turned himself in. Jane squeezed Yin tighter as Todd's parents arrived to pick him up.

Chapter Twenty-Three
Fair is Foul and Foul is Just Plain Nasty

Blog post: *The mouse lives, the birds are free, and the rat gets a second chance.*

Well, dear blog-goers, Souris wasn't dead. He'd just had the wind knocked out of him and some sense shaken into him. He has a renewed respect for the bird kingdom after his near-death encounter with the owl. He reads Shakespeare and looks up at the sky a lot. He's been charged with poisoning birds and turning the cat kingdom into one big stereotype. Extra charges, of going around the laws and trying to take over the world one high-rise at a time, were laid.

It turned out the birds were singing at night because of the construction noise we heard in the daytime. Scientists know that birds sing at night if there is too much noise during the day. Souris had started construction in secret when he'd cleared the brush near some old cottages. He had planned to take over the cottages when he had the land changed from a bird sanctuary to a development site. The birds were competing with the construction noise during the day and kept chirping at night.

Finch was taken to the doctor and diagnosed with tinnitus, a.k.a. ringing in the ears. He also had a good deal of wax build-up. His tinnitus was worse because of the night chirping, caused by his good friend Souris.

There was a big meeting of city council to discuss the use of the land. Everyone wanted to keep it a wilderness area. The cottages on the bird sanctuary land that Souris wanted to destroy were rented to the seniors. In exchange, the seniors would keep the sanctuary wild and help each other. The seniors were happy to be living on their own and back on the land.

Jane's rash cleared up and the seniors only used natural fertilizer. The seniors taught kids how to garden and now the sanctuary is filled with kids. Kitty and Contessa moved into one cottage where they spent many hours fawning over their cat ribbons. Cygnet moved into another cottage while she waited for Aviary to serve out his sentence. Kitty and Cygnet became best friends.

The seniors' lodge, now empty, became a relaxation sanatorium where Finch and Vole were sentenced to live. They took care of the birds that could no longer live in the wild due to hundreds of cats hunting them down and freaking them out. They also cared for some of the cats that didn't get returned to their owners. Finch, Vole, the cats, and birds lived in harmony in the relaxation sanatorium. With the ringing in his ear stopped, Finch enjoyed the chirping of birds again.

Todd wasn't charged, but was punished for being too keen times two and putting the hope of a better summer job over caring about the birds. He was also disciplined for loyalty to culprits. But maybe he didn't know how devious they were because he was a teenager. We all know teenagers think they are smarter than they really are. Jane and I will probably think that until we are teenagers. The punishment for Todd was another summer volunteering at the bird sanctuary, but my mother promised to work with him on the side in the lab. She said he had potential, and I think by that, she meant he would potentially keep the compliments flowing, like free soda refills in an all-you-can-eat restaurant.

Yin was back to normal after her adventure and was cuddled up on my lap as I updated our blog. I closed the laptop. I scratched an itch between her ears as I itched for another mystery.

Discussion Questions

On Shakespeare (aka Mr. Puffy Pants)

Shakespeare was an English poet and playwright who was born in 1564 and died in 1616. Although Cyd and Jane refer to him as the guy with the puffy pants, he was known as England's national poet and the Bard of Avon (he was born in Stratford on Avon). Shakespeare wrote 38 plays, 154 sonnets and several other poems. His plays are comedies, histories and tragedies.

Why, after all these years, is Shakespeare still popular? What are universal themes?

What's a sonnet? And why is he sometimes called the guy with the puffy pants?

On theme

Shakespeare's themes are still important to people in our modern times. There were many themes in the play *Macbeth* that are still relevant today. Themes like greed, ambition, fate, violence, and nature.

What themes from *Macbeth* can you find in Dead Bird through the Cat Door?

Which characters portrayed these themes? Can you point out parts of the book where you can find these themes?

On technology and blogging

Cyd and Jane are active bloggers and they use many forms of technology in their lives. Technology is a part of our every day lives and we use it to make things easier (like a washer and dryer, a fridge, stove and car). Some people think kids today spend too much time with technology (like computers, the internet and video games), and that that type of technology keeps us from interacting with each other.

What technology do you use in your life? How does it help you stay connected to your friends and family? How does it entertain you?

What's a blog? Do you know anyone who blogs? How can a blog be a good outlet for creativity?

How does the blog fit into the story? How did Cyd and Jane use technology to solve the mystery?

On protected areas

There are many protected areas (for example, national parks) all over the world. These areas protect the wildlife and land from development so that we can maintain the natural environment for the plants and animals, and for humans to experience. Why is important to have protected areas? And why is the development of the land (for houses and businesses) limited in these areas?

People have different ideas about what the land should be used for; some people want to develop land and use the resources, and others want to protect the animals and the plant life. How can we balance these ideas so that we can live in harmony with each other and the planet?

On birds and the ecosystem

Birds are an important part of the ecosystem. They eat some insects that harm trees, so the trees stay healthy. Birds spread seeds around so plants will continue to grow. They are beautiful to look at and their chirping on a sunny morning makes us happy. What does it mean to be an important part of the ecosystem? What would happen if one animal, like a bird was no longer around? How would the loss of one animal effect the whole ecosystem? Humans are also an important part of the ecosystem. How does the interconnectedness of humans to the ecosystem relate to the themes in this book?

On cat shows

Cyd and Jane enter Yin in the cat show. Cat owners trim their cats' nails, shampoo their fur, and spritz them with hair spray all in the hopes of winning a ribbon. The cats, meanwhile, sit in cages with velvet cat beds and eat shredded shrimp out of champagne glasses. The more points your cat gets, the better chance it has to win a ribbon and a prestigious title like Supreme Grand Master of cats.

Cyd and Jane thought the world of the cat show was like being in another culture. Each culture has different rules for behaviour, food and dress. How was the cat show scene like being in a different culture?

What makes people want to win? Do you know of a game where there is a hierarchy (for example, you need to get more points to make it higher up in the game)? What's a hierarchy? What are examples of hierarchies in your life? Maybe you participate in sports or dance competitions. Is it like its own culture with rules that may seem strange to outsiders?

On food

In other countries and cultures people eat foods that you might have never heard of. But what may be strange to you may be breakfast to someone in another culture. Cyd and Jane are introduced to some new and unusual foods from Scotland like blood (black) pudding, haggis, and leek soup.

How do things like our culture, our beliefs and our environment (for example, the weather can determine which crops can grow), and our attitudes determine what we eat and how we eat it?

What is the strangest food you have eaten?

Why did you think it was strange?

On balance

The girls' cat is called Yin. In Chinese philosophy, the concept of Yin and Yang is used to describe things that are opposite forces in nature (for example, winter is the yin to summer's yang) and opposites within a whole (like a hot fudge sundae – both hot and cold).

How does the concept of Yin and Yang apply to the characters in the book? Which characters does it apply to?

Acknowledgements

Thanks to the readers (young and old), teachers, and librarians who discovered the first novel in the series *Dead Frog on the Porch* and anxiously awaited the release of this novel, the second in the series. I appreciated the emails.

Thanks to members of the Kensington Writers' Group in Calgary who gave me valuable feedback on the manuscript. You writers rock, as always.

Thanks to the members of my young reader group Teaghan, Logan, Emma, Clara, David and Michael for your insightful advice on an early draft of the manuscript. To my friend Amber, who is an editor trapped in the body of a voracious reader (and recently discovered she's a writer), thanks for your feedback.

I'm happy for the new writer friends I've found through the Society of Children's Book Writers and Illustrators (SCBWI) and The Young Alberta Book Society (YABS). I continue to appreciate the support I get from the writers I know through the Writers Guild of Alberta (WGA), and the Surrey International Writers' Conference (SiWC).

Thanks to Crystal Stranaghan, Publisher and Jared Hunt, Senior Editor of Gumboot Books for their ongoing support of the Megabyte Mystery series, and Melanie Jackson for her copy editing skills. Thanks to Mike Linton for the awesome book cover illustrations.

Thanks to all the members of my large and extended family and friends (longtime and new) for their encouragement and ongoing support of everything I undertake in life.

Thanks, Nancy Drew, fictional character that you are, you were real to many of us young readers who admired your independence and bravery.

about the author
Jan Markley

photo © 2009 Ashley Bristowe

Jan Markley is a writer, author, and presenter living in Calgary, Alberta, Canada. *Dead Bird through the Cat Door* is the second novel in the Megabyte Mystery series. Her debut novel, and the first in the series, is *Dead Frog on the Porch.* Growing up she was a voracious reader of Nancy Drew mysteries and enjoyed visiting the library, where she would stretch her library card to the limit.

Jan previously worked as a print and broadcast journalist. She writes creative non-fiction and has had personal essays published in the Globe and Mail and WestWord. She has a Master of Arts degree in Cultural Anthropology, and enjoys traveling and discovering other cultures.

Check out Jan's website at:
www.deadfrogontheporch.com

Coming Fall 2011 from Gumboot Books

The next megabyte mystery by Jan Markley

Dead Bee in the Sarcophagus

Egyptologists, ancient honey, and King Tut's tomb lead Cyd and Jane on a quest to discover why the bees are disappearing.

The King Tut exhibit is in town, and Cyd and Jane discover that there is ancient honey still encased in the Ivory Pomegranate. Had the boy King Tut planned to eat honey on toast in the afterlife? Can the ancient honey save the bees or will the curse of the tomb destroy the fragile bee population and those who come in contact with it? Everyone wants to get their mitts on the honey and Cyd and Jane's parents get stuck in harm's way. Their annoying friend Todd is, once again, horning in on the mystery.

Cyd and Jane get their sleuth on! To save the Queen Bee and her kingdom, through the boy king and his left over honey, they must navigate the many sticky shades between good and nasty.

visit www.gumbootbooks.com for updates

about gumboot books

Gumboot Books is a socially and environmentally responsible company. We measure our success by the impact we have on the lives and dreams of our authors and illustrators, the impact we have on the environment, and the ways in which we help to enrich the lives of everyone who reads our books.

If you would like to see how we are reducing our ecological footprint, and how we are supporting community numeracy and literacy projects, please visit us online at www.gumbootbooks.com.

ordering information

Please visit us online at

www.gumbootbooks.com

for information on how to order our books.